7 Sister Mysteries

Stage Fright

Ellen Miles

SCHOLASTIC INC.

New York Toronto London Auckland Sydney
Mexico City New Delhi Hong Kong Buenos Aires

For Margaret, Sophie, and Katie

*Many thanks to Kathryn Davis, Morgan Irons,
and Rick Winston*

ISBN 0-439-36005-6

12 11 10 9 8 7 6 5 4 3 2 1   2 3 4 5 6 7/0

Printed in the U.S.A.   40

First Scholastic printing, February 2002

Prologue

It all started so innocently on that snowy March day, with a yellow sign posted on the bulletin board near the cafeteria. It was in the shape of two masks: one happy, one sad. You know, the symbol for drama.

"Got cabin fever?" it read. "Be a part of Drama Club's spring production!"

Underneath that was the date and time of a meeting. I scribbled a note about it in my calendar, thinking it might be fun.

Little did I know that I was about to walk into a whole new world — and into a real-life mystery that would puzzle me, frighten me, and put me in danger. . . .

Chapter One

"'The play's the thing!'" Poppy proclaimed in that stentorian[1] "I'm quoting Shakespeare" voice we all know and love. "More soup, please," he added in a normal tone, holding out his empty bowl.

"'All the world's a stage,'" declared Mom, as if to outdo him. Then she ladled him out another bowl of black bean soup.

"Right," I said.

"*Whatever*," Katherine chimed in.

She and I had just broken the news during dinner on that chilly March night: We were both planning to enter the world of footlights, stage makeup, and curtain calls. That is, we were going to take part in our school play. We weren't the first Parkers to be interested in drama. Oh, no. Mom and Poppy are Shakespeare *nuts*, for one thing. They met in a Shakespeare class in college and went on to marry, move to Cloverdale, Vermont, and have seven daughters. (How very thelyto-

---

[1]stentorian: especially loud. I hope you like interesting words as much as I do! I'll be sharing my collection as we go along.

kous[2] of them.) Check this out: Every one of us has a name from a Shakespeare play. (See what I mean about nuts?)

I'm Ophelia, the middle child. I'm thirteen. Katherine's fourteen. We both go to U-28, the local junior-senior high. We have three younger sisters: Juliet, who's eleven, and Helena and Viola, the nine-year-old twins. Our two older sisters, Miranda (twenty-one) and Olivia (nineteen), don't live at home anymore, but both of them used to be involved in school theater. I remember going to see Miranda dance and sing in *Guys and Dolls*, and Olivia was in almost every play when she was in high school.

"What is it they say? Art imitates life?" Mom asked. "You'll learn a lot about human nature, being part of a play."

"Or is it that life imitates art?" Poppy countered. "I mean, take *Macbeth*. It's set in long-ago Scotland, but the political dealings in that play could be happening right now in Washington, D.C.!"

"Poppy, you're not supposed to say that!" Katherine looked upset.

"Say what?" asked Poppy.

"The name of that play."

"*Macbeth*?"

---

[2]thelytokous: having only female offspring

4

"Shhh!" Katherine shook her head. "It's bad luck. According to theater superstition, you're never supposed to say the title of that play. You call it 'the Scottish play.'"

"Where did you hear *that*?" asked Juliet, helping herself to another piece of bread and smearing it with butter.

"It's common knowledge." Katherine tossed her hair. "If you say that title, your play will be cursed."

"That's ridiculous!" Juliet's never shy about speaking her mind.

"Maybe," said Katherine. "But why risk it?"

"It's too late now, anyway," I pointed out. "Poppy said it. I guess we'll find out whether it's superstition or not."

We found out, all right.

And believe me, I'll never say — that play's name — again.

Chapter Two

"Oh, my God!" whispered my friend Emma Stone when we walked into the auditorium after last bell the next day. "Look who's here."

There were a *ton* of people there for auditions, everyone who was in any way interested in being involved in the play, but I knew who she meant. Down near the stage, sitting at the piano that nestles into the curve on the right side, were Sarabeth Spencer and Travis Mitchell.

Travis was playing, and the two of them were singing a duet, this completely romantic ballad that's all over the radio these days. "When Your Eyes Met Mine," it's called. They sounded almost as good as the band that recorded the song.

A bunch of other kids were sitting around listening. We joined them, slipping quietly into the second row. "He's *so* gorgeous," Emma whispered in my ear.

Funny. My friends and I aren't like that about guys, normally. Well, maybe Emma a little more than Zoe and I. But for the most part we've made a conscious effort to avoid being boy-crazy. We even made a deal about it, that we'd wait until at least eighth grade before we got into dating and all that. We have enough on our minds, as it is. Anyway, I knew Emma didn't actually have a crush on Travis. She just couldn't help reacting to him the way every girl in school did.

Travis is tall, with shiny dark brown hair that sort of flops into his eyes in this incredibly appealing way. He has a slow, warm smile and chocolaty brown eyes, and he always dresses in clean blue jeans and a sparkling white button-down shirt. He and Sarabeth are both seniors, and they're, like, the unofficial king and queen of U-28.

They look great together: Sarabeth also has shiny brown hair, which she wears in a long, thick French braid down her back. She's tall and thin and always smiling, and the fact that her nose is ferntickled[3] makes her seem less perfect but even more pretty, if that makes sense. Everybody likes Sarabeth. She's not stuck-up at all or popular in the usual superficial way. She's just nice. To everyone. She says thank-you to the lunch ladies and helps seventh graders who can't find their lockers, and she's always in the paper as "Volunteer of the Year" at the animal shelter or the soup kitchen. Oh, and like Travis, she's an awesome athlete.

Anyway, if I sound like I'm gushing, I'm not.

[3]ferntickled: freckled

Well, maybe I am, a little. It's just that it's not too often that seventh graders like me and Emma get a chance to mix with the celebrities of our school. It was kind of neat to have the chance to watch those two up close.

We weren't the only ones watching, either. There were kids clustered around the piano and a bunch of people sitting on the stage. Even the one adult there was listening, a big burly guy with a red beard who nodded in appreciation when Travis and Sarabeth nailed a tricky bit of harmonizing.

Emma elbowed me and nodded to our right, down the row of seats. "Isn't that the new guy?" she whispered. "The one in your homeroom? He's in my math class, too."

I turned to look — and blushed when I caught the guy looking right back at me. I turned back to Emma. "Yup," I told her. "His name's PJ, or JT, or something. Just initials, no name. Maybe it's JP? I'm not sure. Anyway, his last name's Okazaki. I know that."

"I like his hair," Emma said.

"It's — unusual," I said. "But I like it, too." Mr. Initials had straight black hair snaking down his back in a long, thick braid. I snuck another peek. This time, he wasn't looking at me. Along with everyone else, he was watching Katherine make her entrance.

Not too many girls at U-28 would try to steal attention from Sarabeth and Travis. But Katherine has guts. She may be a lowly eighth grader, but she's not about to fade into the background. She waltzed right down the center aisle with three guys following her. Katherine rarely goes anywhere without several boys; it's like she's her own little solar system, where she's the sun and the guys are the planets. She planted herself in the middle of the front row, shook back her hair, and applauded politely along with everyone else as Sarabeth and Travis finished their song.

"That was excellent!" said Ms. LaRocque, who had appeared at a side door just as the song was ending. She'd put down the big blue plastic box she was carrying, and she was clapping, too. "Bravo! If we didn't have so much to do today, I'd ask for an encore, but it'll have to wait." She ran up the stairs to the stage, looked out at us, and smiled.

"Welcome to the theater," she said, holding out her arms as if to hug all of us at once.

I couldn't help smiling back at her. Ms. La-Rocque is new: She just started teaching at U-28 in January. But she already has a reputation as the coolest, nicest teacher in school. She was a big part of the reason I'd decided to work on this play. I didn't have any classes with her, but I'd seen her in the halls, skimming along gracefully as if she had on Rollerblades under the long, floaty dresses she always wears. She's a small person, but you can't help noticing her: Her beach-glass blue eyes and long, coppery curls make her stand out, and she's always laughing this surprisingly deep, rich laugh as she talks with other teachers or kids.

"For those who don't know me yet, I'm Madeleine LaRocque. If you stick around to work on this play, you'll call me Maddie. We won't have time for formalities." She came to the front of the stage and sat down, swinging her legs over the edge. "Today's agenda is auditions," she said. "But I wanted everyone to come, whether you're planning on getting the lead" — there was some nervous laughter at that — "or planning to help Sal here build scenery." She gestured to the big red-bearded guy, and he stepped forward to take a little mock bow.

"Sal Sponelli," Ms. LaRocque said, introducing him. "He's a great carpenter and a good friend. We go way back, Sal and I. We met during a production of *West Side Story* down in Boston. Of course, he wasn't a carpenter then. He was in the orchestra, playing a mean sax." She smiled at him. "Anyway, he was the one who inspired me to come to Vermont. He grew up in Cloverdale, and he never got tired of talking about how wonderful it was. He ended up moving back here, and now I'm a Vermontah, too!" She put on a pretty good Vermont accent.

"Anyway," she went on, "Sal will be in charge of all the technical, backstage stuff. I'm sure some of you are here because you're interested in that. I want you all to fill in these audition sheets" — she held up a sheet of paper — "and then we can begin!"

She passed out blank forms, and we all started writing. First there was the usual name-address-phone stuff. Then there were questions about how we wanted to be involved in the play, with boxes to check off for things like actor, stage manager, lighting crew, and costume/makeup crew. I checked off stage manager, even though I was pretty sure they wouldn't give that job to a seventh-grade theater neophyte[4], and set crew. I wasn't at all interested in acting. I'm more the behind-the-scenes type. But I worked on the backstage crew for a production at the elementary school last spring, and I had a great time. I wanted to learn

[4]neophyte: beginner

more about what it took to make a play run smoothly.

Emma checked off scenery. She's an excellent artist, which is why I'd talked her into working on the play. I knew she'd have a great time, and people would be impressed with her talent. I figured it was good for us seventh graders to establish ourselves right away, instead of hiding in a corner, which is what I'm usually tempted to do. But I wasn't about to do it all by myself! I'd tried to convince our friend Zoe to join in, too, but she's always too busy with sports. She was training for track and said there was no way she could fit anything else into her afternoons.

I knew Katherine was checking off actor. Not only that, she was probably going for the lead role. If so, she'd have some stiff competition from Sarabeth, who I knew had played the lead in the past three plays.

We also had to fill in some stuff about our schedules and availability, and whether we'd be willing to rehearse on weekends. People who wanted to act had to fill in their shoe and clothing sizes, for costumes.

While we were working, Ms. LaRocque chatted with Sal up onstage. I watched them, trying to figure out if they were romantically involved. It didn't look like it. They just looked like old friends who were very comfortable with each other.

"Okay, time's up," she announced after a few minutes. "Pass your sheets to the front, if you would. Now, the next thing we're going to do is get to know one another. I've got some little exercises I want us to try. They're known as theater games."

A girl in the front row sat up a little and raised her hand. I recognized her. Blond, lots of makeup. The type my friends and I call a stewardess. She was a junior. "Ms. LaRocque?" she asked.

"Maddie," she corrected. "Yes?"

"I'm Ashleigh Durham," said the girl. "I'll be stage managing."

Ms. LaRocque — Maddie — raised an eyebrow.

"I mean, I always have in the past," Ashleigh said quickly, realizing she'd jumped ahead a little. "Anyway, Ms. Bixby never made nonactors do theater game stuff. So, should we have a separate meeting?"

Maddie smiled. "I think you'll find that I do things a little differently from Ms. Bixby," she said. "For today, I want everybody to participate. It's important that we all feel like a team, whether we have a starring role or never set foot onstage."

Ashleigh sank back down in her seat.

Emma poked me. "I hope we don't have to do anything embarrassing," she whispered.

"Everyone up onstage," said Maddie, opening her arms wide again.

Emma and I walked up the short flight of stairs on the left side of the stage. I had a funny feeling, stepping onto that dark-painted wood floor. For years before I was a student at this school, I'd been coming to plays here. It was always a magical experience to watch the heavy red velvet curtains rise and see the scenery and the brightly costumed actors standing there, ready to take the audience to another place or time. Now I was on that same stage, about to be part of that same magic. I felt a delicious little chill, and suddenly I couldn't wait to find out what was going to happen next.

I didn't have to wait long.

"Okay, let's form a circle for our first game," announced Maddie. "It's called the Name Game, and hopefully it will give us a chance to learn one another's names. I'm going to say my name and show you one of my common mannerisms, something I do all the time. The person to my right will repeat my name and imitate my mannerism, and add his or her own name and mannerism. We'll go all the way around the circle a couple of times, until we all feel like we've known one another for years!"

A few people groaned, but everybody was smiling. It was hard not to around Maddie.

"So. I'm Maddie," she said. "And I do *this* when I'm thinking." Looking toward the ceiling — or rather toward the complicated-looking machinery that hung above the stage — she twirled a lock of hair on her finger.

Ashleigh happened to be standing next to her. "Okay," she said. "You're Maddie, and you do this." She pretended to twirl a lock, which wasn't easy because her hair was pulled back in a tight bun. Everybody giggled. "And I'm Ashleigh, and I do this" — she put a hand on one hip and puffed out her lips in a frustrated sigh — "when I have to do things I don't want to do." She looked at Maddie, almost as if she were daring her to respond.

Maddie just smiled. "Nice," she said. "Next?"

To Ashleigh's right was a boy with brown hair in a mushroom cut, with bangs that fell so far over his black-rimmed glasses that he looked a little like a sheepdog. He was staring down at the floor.

"Next?" Maddie prompted again.

He glanced at her, then quickly down at the floor again. "You're Maddie," he mumbled, so softly I could barely hear him, "and you do this." He touched his hair. "And she's Ashleigh and she does this." He patted his hip. Then he stopped.

"And?" Maddie asked.

15

"I'm Nathan," he finally said. "And I do this." He kicked his foot, as if kicking a rock. "When I'm nervous." Sarabeth was next, but he didn't even glance her way. I saw a deep red flush working its way up his neck.

The game went on, with everybody taking a turn, until we'd all loosened up a little. By the time we went around the circle again, people were laughing and doing exaggerated versions of one another's mannerisms. I showed how I crack my thumb knuckle, and Emma did a neck-roll that she learned in dance class and always does when she's feeling tense. That boy TJ (I finally figured out those initials!) pushed his hair behind his ears. Katherine tossed hers back. A girl named Mel with a bleached-blond buzz cut and metallic blue fingernails gave us an excellent lip-curling sneer.

After that, we played a few other games. In one we had to pair off and interview each other for three minutes, then report on the person we'd interviewed. I got paired with Sarabeth, of all people! I found out that she hates raspberry Jell-O, has a dog named Spike, has never traveled outside of Vermont, and wants to be a veterinarian.

Emma got TJ and learned almost nothing. It seemed like he gave her joke answers to all her questions; the only real things she got out of him were that he'd moved here from a small town near

Seattle, Washington, and that he once ate escargot[5]. And I'm not so sure about the escargot.

In another game, we had to lie on the floor. It was dusty, but I didn't care. Maddie led us through some quick relaxation exercises, then told us to visualize a happy time and place. On the count of three, we all had to scream out a word that defined that place. It was hilarious. Emma yelled, "BenandJerry's!" which meant she'd been thinking about ice cream. I yelled "Pearl Street!" because I was thinking about staying at Olivia's apartment in Burlington, one of my favorite things to do. TJ, who ended up lying near me, yelled what I thought was "shopping!" That seemed a little weird, but I couldn't exactly ask him to explain, since we were already on to the next game, which involved making up a story with each person contributing one word.

When that game ended, Maddie congratulated us all on "surviving." "Now, on to the big stuff," she said. "It's time for auditions."

---

[5]escargot: snails, cooked French style. Ugh.

Chapter Three

"I'd like everyone interested in acting to sit in this section of seats," said Maddie, gesturing to the rows on the right. "Everybody who's interested in helping out in other ways will serve as our audience for now. You can sit over there." She pointed to the seats on the left.

We all filed down the stairs from the stage, sorting ourselves out into groups. Katherine sat with the actors, as I knew she would. I thought I saw TJ hesitate for a second as he watched her walk to the right, but he ended up in the nonactor section, a couple of rows in front of me and Emma. Sal sat with Maddie in the front row. Sarabeth and Travis picked seats near them. Ashleigh plopped herself in the front row of our section, while Mel, the one with the spiky blond 'do, sat down in back of Sarabeth and Travis.

The biggest surprise was that boy Nathan, the one who seemed so incredibly shy. He tripped going down the stairs and nearly fell, and when he caught himself he blushed deep red and looked around as if to see if anyone had been watching. Then he straightened up and walked over to the actors' side, nearly tripping again as he walked past Sarabeth and Travis. I turned to Emma and raised my eyebrows. "He's going to *act*?" I said, nodding at him.

She shrugged. "I have a feeling he's crushing out on Sarabeth," she whispered. "I hear love will make you do things you wouldn't normally do."

"Okay, people, let's get started," said Maddie, standing up and turning around to face us. "I have your audition sheets here, and I'll call on each of you aspiring actors in turn. I hope you've prepared a short monologue, as my signs suggested. I'll also give you a script for the play we'll be doing and ask you to read a few lines from some scenes I've chosen."

Sarabeth raised her hand. "What play *are* we doing?"

"Ah!" said Maddie. "Excellent question. I'm so excited about this! Until yesterday, Sal and I had been talking about doing *Don't Drink the Water*, which is a great old standby for drama clubs. But then, last night, I was at the library, poking around in the Vermont section. And I came across *this* gem." She held up a sheaf of paper. "It's an unpublished play by a local playwright. And it's just *perfect* for us."

Sal was staring at her. "What's the playwright's name?" he asked.

"N. P. Ellison," pronounced Maddie, making it sound like she was saying "William Shakespeare." She looked over at Sal, who was having a sudden coughing fit. "Are you okay?" she asked him. "Want some water?"

He waved a hand. "I'm fine," he said. "Please, go on."

"Anyway, Mr. Ellison was from right here in Cloverdale," Maddie said. "He died young, tragically, in a motorcycle accident. But he was brilliant! He would have gone far in the theater. And this play is wonderful. It's called *A Love Like Ours*, and it's a love story between a boy named Sam and a girl named Donna — but it's a *real* love story, because it doesn't end perfectly, with everyone living happily ever after. I think once you read it, you'll all be as excited as I am about giving this play its Cloverdale premiere."

Sal was still coughing, but he waved her off when she gave him a concerned look.

She glanced down at the script in her hand. "I'll make some more copies tonight, but for now we can pass this one around. Now, let's see. Who's first?" She rustled through the pile of audition sheets. "How about — Mel?" She looked around.

Mel bounded up onto the stage. She looked totally comfortable up there, not nervous at all. "I'll be doing a scene from *Funny Girl*," she said. And she swung right into it. She spoke clearly and moved around the stage a little and got laughs on all the funny lines. She seemed like a pro. And when Maddie handed her the script from the play we'd be doing, she read off the lines for the second female lead, a character named Veronica, with no hesitation at all. She was obviously an experienced — and talented — actress. Everybody applauded at the end of the scene.

"Nice work," said Maddie, when she was done.

"Cool," said Mel, jumping down off the stage.

"Let's have Katherine next," said Maddie.

I watched Katherine walk confidently up to the stage. I was so glad that for once she and I weren't competing. This time around, she could do her thing and I could do mine, and we wouldn't be in each other's way at all.

Katherine aced her monologue, a passage from — what else — *The Taming of the Shrew* (that's the play her namesake is in). She also did really well with the script Maddie gave her, reading the part of Donna.

When she was done, Maddie looked at Sarabeth. "Next?" Travis rose to let Sarabeth out of her seat. "What about you, Travis?" asked Maddie. "I don't seem to have your sheet."

21

"Oh, I'm not trying out, ma'am," Travis said. He always sounds like some character in an old-fashioned movie. He's superpolite and so sweet. He treats Sarabeth like a princess. Once when we got let out early for a snowstorm, I saw him shovel a path through the snow in the parking lot so she could walk to his car without getting her feet wet. "I'm just here to support Sarabeth."

"How nice," said Maddie. "Well, I'm sure we can use your help if you're going to be around. Mr. Wilson tells me you're one of his most talented students." Mr. Wilson is the shop teacher. He's a pretty old-fashioned guy himself. He's always coming out with these corny sayings, and he dresses like Mr. Rogers on TV, in sneakers and a cardigan.

Travis ducked his head. "Glad to, ma'am," he said.

Maddie smiled. "You don't have to 'ma'am' me quite so much," she said. "In fact, I'd prefer not being 'ma'amed' at all."

"Yes, ma'a —" Travis stopped himself. "Okay, Ms. LaRocque," he said. He kissed Sarabeth on the cheek. "Good luck, sweetie," he said, sending her up to the stage.

"I've prepared a monologue from *Saint Joan*," Sarabeth said when she was standing up there facing us. "It's about Joan of Arc," she added helpfully. "The girl who dressed up like a soldier and eventually got burned at the stake."

"Wonderful." Maddie nodded approvingly. "Go on."

Sarabeth took a deep breath. Then she drew herself up and started to speak. "'. . . you promised me my life, but you lied.'"

She went on with this whole impassioned speech about how awful it would be to be locked away. The speech finished with some awesome, powerful lines about how she (Joan) couldn't live if she were in prison, if she couldn't hear the "wind in the trees" and the "larks in the sunshine."

By that time, Sarabeth had everybody in the auditorium leaning forward in their seats, completely involved in what she was saying. I felt tears springing into my eyes — she was that good.

She finished and there was a moment of silence before the first person started clapping. I happened to notice that it was Nathan, not Travis, who led the applause. Sarabeth smiled at him from the stage, and I saw that flush rise again on the back of his neck.

A few other people tried out. Some of them hadn't remembered or bothered to learn monologues, and I could tell Maddie wasn't impressed. Others stumbled through their reading, stiff and fake-sounding. But everybody, no matter how pathetic, got a round of hortatory[6] applause, usually led by Maddie. Then it was Nathan's turn.

I almost didn't want to watch. It was going to be painful to see him stumble up onto the stage and mumble his way through some boring speech.

Sure enough, he dropped the script Maddie handed him three times and tripped twice on his way to the stage. In between picking up himself and the script, he kept pushing his glasses back in this distracted way as they slid down his nose.

Finally, he was standing in the center of the stage. He put the script down on the table next to him and cleared his throat. Once, twice, three times. "Um," he said.

"Go on," Maddie prompted. "Tell us about the monologue you'll be delivering."

"It's — um — from *Romeo and Juliet*," Nathan mumbled. "You know. By, like, Shakespeare."

"Wonderful!" Maddie sat back and crossed her arms, an eager look on her face. I slid down in my seat, cringing.

Nathan took off his glasses and put them on the table. He turned his back for a moment and brushed back his hair with one hand. Then he turned around to face us.

[6]hortatory: giving strong encouragement

24

And something amazing happened. Nathan *became* Romeo. That's the only way I can describe it. Suddenly, he looked completely different. Taller, more confident. Handsome, even. And he spoke loudly and clearly and — beautifully.

"'But soft,'" he said, "'what light through yonder window breaks? It is the east, and Juliet is the sun. Arise, fair sun, and kill the envious moon, who is already sick and pale with grief, that thou her maid are far more fair than she. . . . '"

He went on with what has to be one of the most romantic speeches in the world, the one that takes place when Romeo is standing beneath Juliet's balcony. He was so convincing that you could almost *see* Juliet above him, framed by pink climbing roses.

"'See,'" he finished, "'how she leans her cheek upon her hand! O, that I were a glove upon that hand, that I might touch that cheek!'"

Suddenly, Sarabeth rose out of her seat and pushed past Travis, who looked up at her, surprised. "'Aye, me!'" she said.

Juliet's line.

Nathan didn't miss a beat. He looked down at Sarabeth and, without blushing or stammering, went on, "'She speaks; O, speak again, bright angel!'"

"'Romeo, Romeo,'" said Sarabeth, making her

way up the aisle toward the stage, "'wherefore art thou, Romeo?'"

Nathan's mouth opened, but no words came out. His face turned white. He looked like a trapped animal. "Th-that's all I learned," he said, grabbing his glasses off the table and shoving them back onto his face.

"Wow," said Sarabeth. "Wow." She looked up at him and began to applaud, and everybody else joined in. Everybody but Travis, that is. He still looked slightly stunned. Nathan clearly wanted to bolt off the stage.

"Sarabeth, as long as you're almost up there, why don't you and Nathan read a scene together?" asked Maddie. "Try page" — she looked at her script — "twelve. Act One, Scene Two. Where Donna and Sam are sitting on her front porch."

Sarabeth climbed the stairs and joined Nathan onstage. He picked up the script, dropped it, picked it up again. Gently, she took it from him and held it for both of them. They started to read, and it was like the same thing happened all over again. The scene was a sweet one, where the two young lovers are talking. Nathan *became* Sam, a confident boy who knows exactly how he feels about the girl sitting next to him.

"'Donna,'" he said, "'There's something I've been meaning to tell you. Something big.'"

"'What is it, Sam?'" asked Sarabeth.

"'Just this,'" he said. "'You're the best thing that ever happened to me. You're my moon and stars, And I want us to be together forever.'"

"'Oh, Sam,'" Sarabeth answered. "'I feel the exact same way. But we're only in high school. We can't know what might happen in our future.'"

They went on for a while, until Sal nudged Maddie and she told them to stop. Then, once again, Nathan returned to his regular old clumsy, shy self, and he and Sarabeth walked off the stage to thunderous applause and whistles.

There was very little question in anybody's mind. Nathan and Sarabeth were obviously going to play Sam and Donna.

Everybody knew it. I could see it on Mel's and Katherine's faces, which showed a mixture of admiration and envy. (I'd be envious, too, if I were an actress competing with Sarabeth!)

Travis, meanwhile, looked as if he were bursting with pride.

And Nathan? Anybody else would have looked pretty pleased with themselves. But Nathan looked terrified. His look said, *Oh, no! Now I'm going to have to do this!*

"Well!" said Maddie, standing up to face us. "This has been quite an afternoon. I think we've done everything we need to do today, so I'll let you go. The cast list and assignment of stage crew will be posted tomorrow, by noon, on the Stage-lights bulletin board. That's the one just outside the rear exit of the auditorium, for those who don't know. If you're involved in the play, you'll become very, very familiar with that board. You'll need to check it on a daily basis, because it's where I'll post schedules, notes, notices about meetings, and any-thing else I want everyone to know."

She thanked us all for coming. "If you audi-tioned but *don't* get a part," she added, "please don't be discouraged. There'll be plenty more plays. And we'd love to have you work on sets, props, or costumes, if you're willing. I think you'll find that working in the theater is incredibly excit-ing and rewarding, no matter what your role."

It sounded good, and I know she meant it, but I could tell from some people's faces — including Katherine's — that if they didn't get a role they weren't about to lower themselves by working be-hind the scenes. For some people, theater is about being onstage, and there are no two ways about it. I knew those people wouldn't sleep well that night, waiting to see that cast list.

Chapter Four

"It's up!" Emma grabbed me as we passed in the hall between third and fourth period the next day.

"The cast list?" I asked.

She tapped her watch. "It's twelve-fifteen. It *must* be up." She pulled me along. "I'm dying to know who got what, aren't you?"

We only had a couple of minutes if we didn't want to be late for our next classes, so we rushed toward the Stagelights bulletin board. On the way, we passed TJ rushing in the opposite direction.

"Hey, who got the leads?" Emma called out to him.

He looked over at us, shook his head, and kept going.

"Weird," commented Emma.

"We'll see for ourselves soon enough," I told her. "Maybe he didn't really recognize us from yesterday. He's new. He's meeting a lot of people at once."

We raced around the corner and almost ran into Katherine. "Did you get a part?" I asked her.

"Who can tell?" she answered. She looked a little mad.

"What do you mean?" I looked over her shoulder, trying to make out the cast list. But it was hidden by the crowd that had gathered around the bulletin board.

"See for yourselves," she said. "I have a class to get to."

Emma and I worked our way to the front of the crowd. People were making comments like, "Why would somebody do that?" and "That's creepy."

I still couldn't figure out what was going on — until I saw it.

The paper was tacked to the middle of the board. CAST LIST it said on top. But that was all you could read. The rest of it had been sprayed with green metallic paint, so heavily applied that it blocked out any printing underneath it.

The paint didn't cover the whole page, though. The margin was still white. Except for the red writing, that is. The writing that said,

BREAK A LEG!

Chapter Five

Emma and I — and a bunch of other people — were still gaping at the ruined sign when Maddie LaRocque hurried up, along with Sal. "Oh, really!" she said when she saw the defaced list. She pulled it down and handed it to Sal, who crumpled it up. Meanwhile, Maddie was putting up another copy of the list. "There!" she said. "Now, Sal came to take me to lunch. I'll be back in a half hour, and I sure hope that list is still here by then!" She smiled around at us. "Congratulations to you all," she added. "Everybody who tried out got a part, even if it wasn't exactly the one they wanted. I think we're going to have a fabulous time doing this play!" With that, she glided off down the hall, Sal ambling along beside her.

Everybody pushed in closer to see the list. I joined them, trying to ignore the feeling of uneasiness that the scrawled message had given me.

I searched for my name. "Wow!" I said when I saw it. "Assistant stage manager! Cool." Just what I'd wanted. I'd be working with Ashleigh, who had been named stage manager, just as she'd assumed. I saw her turning away from the bulletin board, a satisfied look on her face.

"And I'm on sets." Emma pointed to her name. "And stage crew."

Right under Emma's name was TJ's. So he'd be working backstage, too. Maybe we'd get to know him a little better.

Once we'd found our names, we took a second to see who'd gotten which roles. "I knew it!" Emma said, pointing at the top of the list. "Sarabeth got Donna, and Nathan got Sam. They'll be perfect."

"Check it out!" I pointed to another name. Katherine had gotten the part of Veronica, the second lead! Not too bad for an eighth grader. Mel was going to play Donna's mother, and she'd also be an understudy for some other female parts. (She didn't look too thrilled about that.) A boy named Duncan who had come to auditions late would be understudy for the boys. A bunch of other people were listed to play smaller parts. Maddie was right; there was a part for everyone.

At the bottom of the list, Maddie had added a note: THERE WILL BE A BRIEF MEETING TODAY FOR EVERYONE INVOLVED IN THE PLAY, IMMEDIATELY AFTER LAST BELL!!

*   *   *

32

I got out of my last class a little early that day, so I headed for the auditorium. Maybe Maddie or Ashleigh would be there, and I could find out more about what my job would be as assistant stage manager. To be honest, I had some trepidation[7] about what was going to be expected of me.

When I opened the auditorium doors, the first thing I noticed was the music. Waves of beautiful, complicated notes tumbled into the air, reminding me of Poppy's favorite CD of piano sonatas by Mozart. But this wasn't Mozart. And it wasn't a CD. I walked into the dimly lit auditorium and discovered that nobody else was there yet; nobody except TJ, who was sitting alone at the piano, producing that incredible sound.

His eyes were squinched shut, and his hands moved like lightning over the keys while his feet pumped at the pedals. The notes rang out, filling the auditorium. I stopped in my tracks to watch. He didn't even have any music in front of him. I couldn't imagine ever being able to play like that, much less without music to follow. That meant he had all those notes in his head! And this wasn't some simple Top 40 song, like the one Travis had been playing the day before. This was the real stuff.

I listened as the music grew and changed, cir-

[7]trepidation: fear, apprehension

cling around to the same simple theme again and again. Finally, TJ pounded out three loud chords — and one final soft one. The piece was over. He sat with his head bowed, eyes still closed, his hands resting gently on the keys.

I walked a little closer. "Wow," I said softly. "That was — amazing."

He looked up at me, surprised. "What are *you* doing here?" he asked, a little foggily. It was as if he'd just woken up from a nap.

"I'm here for the meeting. What was that music? And how did you learn to play like that?"

He shrugged. "Chopin," he said. "And lots of lessons."

"Chopin!" I said. "*That's* what you said yesterday. Chopin, not shopping! When we were doing that visualize-a-happy-time thing."

He shrugged again. "I guess," he said. "I don't remember." He closed the lid over the piano's keys and spun around on the stool, not meeting my eyes.

"My sister would *love* to hear you play," I said, thinking of Juliet. She's been taking piano lessons forever.

"The blond?" TJ asked. "The one who's playing Veronica?"

How did he know Katherine was my sister? "How did you know —?"

Another shrug. "Your name's Parker. So's hers."

Just then, the doors to the auditorium flew open, the lights came on, and kids started pouring in. "Not Katherine," I told him. "Juliet."

"I suppose there's a Miranda at home, too?" he asked.

I raised my eyebrows. A boy who knew his Shakespeare! Then I just nodded. "And a Viola, a Helena, and an Olivia," I confessed.

TJ's mouth dropped open. I'm used to that reaction when I tell people about my humongous family, so I just smiled.

Then Maddie arrived. She ran right up onto the stage and greeted us. "Ready to get to work?" she asked happily. "I apologize for that little incident this afternoon. Someone clearly felt the need to pull a prank. We'll ignore it and move on." She bent to lift a pile of photocopied scripts out of her big plastic box. "Ashleigh and Ophelia, can you help me pass these out? There's one for everyone."

While we passed out the scripts, Maddie announced that she expected all of us to read the play that night. "We'll have our first read-through tomorrow," she said. "That means everyone needs to be here right after last bell again. We'll go through the entire play so everyone has a sense of the story. After that, we'll continue to have read-throughs, but we won't necessarily need every actor every day. Your stage managers and I will break down the scenes and make a schedule, which we'll post on the Stagelights board. You will be expected to not only attend every rehearsal you're scheduled for, but to be on time and be prepared. If you have a conflict, make sure to let the stage managers know. Stage crew, tech people, and people working on sets will answer to Sal. In fact, those folks can meet with Sal right now, while I go over a few things with the actors. Ashleigh, why don't you bring Ophelia up to speed on what you two will be doing. Any questions?" She flashed a smile.

Wow. Maddie was nice, but she was no pushover. I could tell she was organized and serious and that she expected a lot from us. I liked that.

Here's what I *didn't* like so much: When Ashleigh and I sat down to talk, I started to get the definite feeling that she wasn't going to be around much. "I want this stage manager credit on my record 'cause it looks good for college applications. But I just got a part-time job at the mini-mart," she told me. "And I have *tons* of homework lately. Plus a dance concert coming up that I'm rehearsing for at least twice a week." She gave me a little shrug. "Guess you'll be covering for me some."

"But — I don't know anything about how to be a stage manager," I told her, feeling slightly panicked.

"Basically," she said, "the stage manager is the director's right hand. You make sure all the actors get to all the rehearsals, you take notes when the director is blocking, you call lighting and sound cues, you prompt during rehearsals, you make sure the stage is ready with props and sets and stuff. And during performances, you basically run the show backstage. You're the one who gets to say when the curtain goes up in the beginning and when it goes down at the end. You'll pick it up fast."

I stared at her, totally overwhelmed.

She waved a hand casually. "Don't worry. There's nothing to it."

And that, dear reader, turned out to be the world's biggest lie.

Chapter Six

"So? What do you think?" asked Emma as we left the auditorium.

"I think I might have just bitten off more than I can chew," I said.

"Huh?" She gave me a weird look.

"It's an expression of Poppy's," I told her. "It means —"

"That you're in over your head," TJ said lightly, coming up behind us. "Don't worry — you can handle it."

"How do you know?" I asked.

He looked serious all of a sudden. "My dad always says I'm a fine judge of character. I can tell you're the kind of person who can take care of a lot of things at once."

"Well — thanks." Interesting. He was right, I guess. It's what I'm best at. Good old reliable Ophelia. I may not be as beautiful as Katherine or as tenacious[8] as Juliet or as athletic as Helena, but I am the one people turn to when they need someone to count on.

---

[8]tenacious: stubborn, somebody who really hangs in there

I asked Emma if she wanted to come over for dinner, and she went to call her mom to see if it was okay. I noticed TJ still standing there, looking down at his black high-tops. "Would you like to come, too?" I asked, without giving myself a chance to think about it. "You can meet my sisters. Olivia might even be there. She's my favorite."

"Really?" he asked. "Will there be enough? Won't your parents mind?"

"It's fine," I told him. "We're having spaghetti. It's Helena's and Viola's turn to help with dinner, and they'll just throw some extra pasta into the pot." We started walking to the door. "Do you want to call home?" I asked.

"Don't need to. My mom works late tonight. I'd be cooking for myself anyway."

"What about your dad?" I asked, feeling a little nosy.

"Oh — he works late, too," TJ said quickly. "Lots of nights."

We caught the late bus home (our school is just outside of town, a little too far to walk, especially on cold nights like that one) and got off a block from our house. Katherine, who'd been on the bus, too, lagged behind talking to her friend Amy, but Emma and TJ and I hurried on ahead.

"I like your house," TJ said as we came up the walk.

"Thanks," I said. I like our house, too. It's a big old rambling farmhouse, with an attached barn and three porches: one in front, one in back, and one on the second floor. It's a white house, with green shutters and big flower gardens in front, though those were still covered with snowdrifts. March in Vermont is still pretty wintry; we always get a couple of big snowstorms before the month is out. That night there were lights on all through the house. The homey, golden glow that shone through the windows made me feel happy to be coming home.

I brought Emma and TJ into the kitchen and introduced TJ to Helena, Viola, Poppy, and Bob, our dog. Bob is always in the kitchen when anyone is cooking, groaking[9] underfoot, hoping for scraps. He came over to sniff TJ and get his ears scratched. Then he went back to his spot by Helena's feet.

"Pleased to meet you," said Poppy, wiping his hands on a dish towel before sticking one out for a shake. "Hope you like garlic."

TJ sniffed the steamy, fragrant air. "It smells great," he said.

"Can we help?" Emma asked.

---

[9]groak: to stare at someone who's eating (or cooking, in this case), hoping for a handout

Poppy beamed. He likes Emma a lot. "Nice of you to ask, Ms. Emma. How about if you three set the table? It's Katherine's turn, but dinner's ready and she's not here yet. She can help clear instead."

Miranda and Steve (Miranda's fiancé — they've been together for years, so he's already practically part of the family) showed up while we were putting out the silverware. Miranda had come straight from work, and she was still in uniform. When TJ saw her, he dropped a handful of spoons onto the table, making a big clatter.

"Your sister's a cop?" TJ whispered to me after I'd introduced him.

I nodded. "She's going to be a detective someday. My mom works for the police, too. She's a dispatcher."

"What about your dad?" TJ asked. "What does he do?"

I told TJ about Poppy's job, working for the Federal Aviation Administration. "When there's a plane crash somewhere, he has to go investigate. Between crashes, he gets to work mostly at home." I was just about to ask TJ about his parents and what they did, when Olivia turned up. "Class got canceled tonight," she said, giving me a hug. "Figured I'd come hang out with the fam."

"Yay!" I said. I introduced her to TJ.

"Nice braid," she told him.

"Thanks." He looked down at the floor and blushed. Then he smiled at her. "I like your hair, too."

Hmm. Score one for TJ. Olivia's hair is frizzy and thick like mine, and she doesn't even *try* to tame it. I love it, but I think most guys would consider her style a little wild.

Just then, Juliet came running down the stairs, and I introduced her, too. "You should hear TJ play piano," I said. "He's awesome."

He blushed some more.

In another few minutes, Mom came home from work, and I introduced TJ one more time. "Good to have you," Mom said. "Have you met everyone?"

"Everyone but Charles and Jenny," I said.

TJ looked totally overwhelmed. "I thought —"

"They're our cats," I explained. "They're probably sleeping upstairs. We'll find them later."

"Cool," he said. "I love cats."

Another point in his favor, I thought. "Do you have one?"

"Used to." He didn't explain further.

"Meanwhile," Poppy said, coming into the dining room carrying a huge bowl of spaghetti, "it's time to eat."

Katherine showed up just in time to slide into

her seat and accept a plate of spaghetti. TJ seemed to perk up when she arrived. His eyes followed her as she shook out her napkin and picked up a fork. Like, fascinating. When we were all served, Viola led off the "daily news" segment of the evening. (It's a Parker family tradition. Every night at dinner we each have to talk for a couple of minutes about something that happened that day.)

"We're doing anagrams in language arts class," she reported. "Did you know the letters of my full name can be rearranged to spell A Brave Solar Pinkie?" Viola loves word games. She's quite a cruciverbalist[10], too. Her full name is Viola Baines Parker. Baines is my mother's maiden name; all of us have it for our middle name.

We all cracked up. "And I'm Risk Banana Peel Here," Helena said, giggling.

"I checked an anagram website one time," I reported. "The best anagram for my name was Hire Sole Paprika Bean." I turned to TJ. "How about you?" I asked. "What *does* TJ stand for, anyway?"

He took a huge bite of spaghetti and held up a hand to show that his mouth was full and he couldn't talk.

Juliet jumped in. "Can I tell my news?" she

[10]cruciverbalist: someone who loves doing crossword puzzles

asked, and told us about a report she'd been working on. She could have rattled on all night, but I held up my hand. "My turn?" I asked.

"Don't know," Poppy said. "TJ, when's your birthday?"

TJ stared at him.

"We go from oldest to youngest one day, youngest to oldest the next," Poppy explained. "I need to know your birthday to know if you go before or after Ophelia and Emma."

Guests are not excused from our family tradition. TJ looked a little panicked.

"Um, it'll be in August," he muttered finally.

"Aha!" said Poppy. "Your turn!"

Just then, the light over the table went out. We all groaned.

"Arrgh!" said Poppy. "Not again!"

TJ looked up at the light. "It goes out by itself?" he asked.

"Sometimes," Poppy admitted. "I've tried to figure it out, but I can't seem to fix it."

Poppy's a great gardener and a terrific cook, but he's not so handy with stuff like hammers and nails and electricity and plumbing.

"Where's the fuse box?" asked TJ.

Poppy and he took off for the basement. A few minutes later, the light came back on. When TJ and Poppy came back up, we all applauded.

"This is a very handy fellow," Poppy reported. "Knows his way around a fuse box." He patted TJ on the shoulder.

"Do I still have to give news?" TJ asked.

"Not if you don't want to," Mom said. "You've earned your supper." She smiled at him and passed the spaghetti.

That night, after TJ and Emma left, I got everybody's reactions. "He's nice," said Helena. "Is he going to be your boyfriend?"

I yelped. "Helena! He's just a friend! I mean — he's not even that, yet. I barely know him."

"Calm down," said Mom. "Whatever he is, Helena's right. He's very nice."

"And cute," Olivia added.

"And talented." Juliet had let TJ try out her electronic keyboard, and he'd impressed everyone by playing a ragtime tune with complicated rhythms.

"I don't know," Katherine said. "There's something about him. Something he's . . . hiding. Or maybe he's just kind of weird. I'm just not sure I trust him."

Was Katherine jealous because I'd made a new friend? Or — I couldn't help wondering — was she a better judge of character than I was?

Chapter Seven

Later that night, after Miranda, Steve, and Olivia had taken off, I settled myself on the living-room couch to read through the script. Katherine had taken hers upstairs to read.

Maddie was right. It was a good play. I was impressed that a local author had written it. It was set in the 1950s, in Butterfield, a small New Hampshire town, and it was about two teenagers, Sam and Donna. Here's the story: In Act One, they fall in love. Sam has dreams of becoming an artist. He's very talented, and Donna encourages his dreams. But Sam's father wants him to join the family business and be a plumber.

In Scene Three, Sam and Donna pledge their undying love for each other. And Sam tells Donna his secret: He's applied to a New York City art school.

In Scene Four, Sam stands up to his father. He's been accepted at the art school, and he's going to go. And in Scene Five, he tells Donna he's leaving and begs her to come with him. He even proposes marriage! Donna is torn. She loves Sam, but she's not ready to leave their small town. Her mother is ill, and Donna is needed at home. Sam tells her it doesn't matter. He'll be back on his breaks, and one day maybe Donna will join him in the big city, or maybe he'll come back to live in Butterfield.

I have to admit I teared up a bit reading that scene. It was heart-wrenching to see Sam and Donna split apart!

Anyway, in Act Two Sam goes to New York, where he enrolls in art school and meets its benefactor, a very rich socialite named Mrs. Drysdale. She sees his talent and takes him under her wing. He attends parties and dinners at her house, where he gets to know (uh-oh!) her daughter, the pulchritudinous[11] Veronica. Mrs. Drysdale is clearly trying to do a little matchmaking, and while Sam is reluctant at first, he eventually falls for Veronica.

Meanwhile, Donna is back in Butterfield, waiting for Sam to return. He means to visit, but doesn't, and he begins to feel more and more guilty. The play shows this part through letters: Donna reads Sam's out loud, and he reads hers. At first, Donna accepts his excuses. But over time she becomes lonelier and less hopeful that he'll return.

In Scene Four, Donna's mother dies — and Sam doesn't show up for the funeral because he has an

[11]pulchritudinous: beautiful

art show he must attend. That's the last straw for Donna. She stops writing to him.

Sam marries Veronica, and time passes. They have children; his art career has its fabulous ups and dismal downs. It's obvious that he and Veronica are not soul mates.

In Act Three, there's a flash-forward to ten years later. Sam has failed as an artist and divorced Veronica. He comes back to Butterfield to try to start his life over again in the family plumbing business, and he and Donna have a big reunion. She's married now, with a family. They meet at a café, and it's almost like old times, the way they connect. Sam begs her to forgive him, and she tells him she already has. In the last scene, they meet again, in the park, and this time Sam begs her to come back to him, to leave her husband and give him a second chance. They kiss — and the play ends.

I put down the script. Whoa! What a story. I thought about what might happen next. Does Donna leave her husband, marry Sam, and live happily ever after with her first, real love? Or does she tell Sam to get lost, leaving him to live with the fact that he'd made the wrong choice so many years before? I liked the way the author left it hanging, so you had to think about it. That way, each person who sees the play can see it in a different way, according to what *they* think happened.

Me? I don't know too much about all that love stuff, only what I've seen in the movies and read in books. But my feeling was that Sam *did* make the wrong choice when he left Donna behind. And he made another wrong choice when he married Veronica. Donna might forgive him, but there's no way she should break up her family and go off with him. Anyway, she's a good person, and she wouldn't do that, no matter how much her first love meant to her.

But what do I know?

One thing I knew for sure was that Maddie had made great choices when she picked her cast. Sarabeth and Nathan were going to be perfect as Donna and Sam, and Katherine — well, nobody could play a spoiled, beautiful socialite's daughter like Katherine could. She was *made* to play Veronica!

Reading the play got me really excited about working on it. Suddenly, I could hardly wait for the next day's rehearsal. I'd already almost forgotten the moment of fear I'd felt when I saw that ruined cast list. Anyway, I wasn't going to let one dumb prank ruin my first big theater experience.

Chapter Eight

"Ever heard the expression 'waiting in the wings'?" Maddie asked us. "Well, this is where it comes from. The wings are where you should be if you have an entrance soon. It's also where we keep the prop table. It's where the stage manager is stationed during performances" — she gestured at a stool — "and where some of you tech people will be working."

It was the next afternoon, and Maddie was giving us a tour of the theater — "Theater 101," she called it. Some of the people in the group had heard and seen it all before, but Maddie had insisted that everyone participate. "The area above us is called the flies," Maddie said, pointing straight up. "Certain scenery gets 'flown' up there when it needs to be out of sight. It hangs, along with some lights, from the battens, those horizontal rods you see. Everything is operated with pulleys, from the fly gallery, here against the backstage wall." I saw TJ checking out the ropes and pulleys, nodding as if he already understood the whole complicated system.

There was a painted backdrop, left over from

the last play. It showed a city street, with stores and apartments and signs. "We'll be painting all new drops," said Sal, who was walking along with us. "Drops are these canvas cloths. We'll also be building and painting some flats, which are wood-framed panels that can stand in as walls."

Maddie led us across the stage to the other wing. "Back here," she said, "in the left wing, we have this tiny room." She unlocked the door and turned on a light. "We'll keep costumes and props for the current play in here."

"Nice decor!" said Mel. She was already scoping out the room. I poked my head inside and saw that the walls in the little, windowless room were covered with graffiti. It seemed like every kid who'd ever been in a play at U-28 had signed that wall. Some kids had long lists of credits under their names. Right away, I spotted Olivia's name. *Olivia Parker*, she'd scrawled in red paint. Underneath her name, in different colors, were the plays she'd done: *Guys and Dolls*, *The Wizard of Oz*, *Arsenic and Old Lace*, *The Tempest*.

I could remember her in every one of those plays. Olivia's a really good actress. Mom always said she had a way of lighting up the stage. "That's my sister," I told Ashleigh, who was standing near me. I pointed to Olivia's name.

"Uh-huh," she said. She looked totally bored.

She must have been in that room a million times before.

Travis found Sarabeth's name and pointed it out proudly. She looked a little embarrassed as he loudly read off her credits. I thought it was sweet of him to tag along on our tour. I heard him say he wanted to "get to know Sarabeth's world."

Maddie showed us around a little more, pointing out the area where sets would be constructed, just offstage, and giving us a tour of the lighting booth, up in the back of the auditorium. "We use headsets to communicate with the tech crew up here," she told us, and I had a vision of myself looking professional and capable, talking into a headset and giving the tech crew orders. Yeah, right. Like I had any idea what I'd be ordering them to do!

Then Maddie led us back to the stage. "Okay, one last thing," she said. She walked to the front of the stage, toward the phantom audience. "Downstage," she said. She walked back toward the backdrop. "Upstage." She walked to her left. "Stage left." And to her right. "Stage right. Note that it's *my* left, and *my* right, not the audience's!" Then she walked to the middle of the stage. "Center stage," she said, holding out her hands. "Got it?"

"Got it," we chorused.

"It gets a little more complicated," she said, "when you add it all together. There's down right, down center, down left. Up right, up center, up left." She walked to the back — I mean upstage — and left. "If I ask Nathan to cross from up left to down right, this is what I'm looking for." She walked diagonally across the stage. "But I might not want him to take a straight line like that. It usually looks better from the audience if you put a little curve in your path." She waved a hand. "More on that later. Stage crew also needs to know stage directions, so they can put things in the right place, and the lighting crew obviously needs to light the right area." She checked her watch. "One last thing," she said. "Very basic. Actors need to act *to the audience*. That means you don't turn your back on them, and you don't talk into the wings. You face forward or give them a three-quarter view of your face" — she demonstrated by turning slightly away from us — "and you *project* and *enunciate*[12] so that the people in the back rows can hear and understand you."

She gave us a sudden, bright smile. "You actors will be hearing that over and over," she said. "Okay! That's it for the tour. I think Sal wants to

[12] enunciate (I looked this up later, even though I had a fairly good idea of what it meant): to say words carefully, pronouncing each letter clearly

meet with all the backstage people, and the rest of us need to get started on our read-through. Ashleigh and Ophelia, you can join us at the table." She pointed to a table and chairs that had been set up onstage.

As I waved good-bye to Emma and TJ, I saw Duncan tapping Travis on the shoulder. "So your girlfriend's going to be making out with another guy today," he said. "*That* should be fun to watch."

Travis whipped around to face Duncan. His face was serious, his mouth set in a straight line. "That's not going to happen," he said.

"It's in the script!" Duncan didn't know when to quit. Or maybe he hadn't noticed the way Travis's fists were clenched at his sides.

"Whoa, whoa," said Maddie, who'd also overheard. "First of all, Sarabeth and Nathan are *not* going to make out. Yes, there's a kiss in Scene Three, and one at the end of the play, too. But we'll work up to those. I don't expect or need them to actually kiss until dress rehearsal." She raised her voice, so everyone could hear. "People, this is a love story. Get used to it. I don't want any teasing and silliness around that. Understood?" She smiled at Travis. "Remember, it's just a play," she added.

Travis relaxed. "Yes, ma'am," he said.

Maddie rolled her eyes.

"I mean, *Maddie*," he said, giving her that great smile of his.

"Travis," she said, "as long as you're here, can you do me a favor? We're going to need a few more copies of the script. Maybe you could take this down to the office and ask Mrs. Deaver to run some off? If you could wait till they're done, that would be fantastic."

"Glad to help," Travis said. He took the script, blew a kiss to Sarabeth, and headed off.

Ashleigh, who was sitting near me, shook her head and sighed. "If I ever found a boyfriend like that," she said, "I'd *never* let him go."

"All right, then," Maddie said when we were all seated around the big table. "Let's get started. Today we're just going to read straight through the script, with each person taking his or her part. I'm not looking for big character development here; we just want to get a sense of the story, the whole wonderful romance."

Just then, there was a big crash from backstage. "Sal?" she called out. "Everything okay?"

Sal appeared in the wing, looking sheepish. "Sorry," he said. "We'll hold it down, I promise."

Maddie smiled at him. "That's okay," she said. "I expect a certain amount of noise when actors and crew overlap. It's going to happen, with the tight schedule we have." She turned back to us.

"Where was I?" She looked down at her notes. "Oh, right. As far as character development, what I want is for you each to start thinking about your character. How does he walk? How does she sit? Does she have a certain way of talking? Some of these things are in the script: Sarabeth, you might have noticed that Donna often repeats herself when she's nervous. You can start working on that. And Nathan —"

At the sound of his name, Nathan, who had been leaning his chair back on two legs, suddenly looked up. His eyes had this frightened look, "like a deer in headlights" as Vermonters say. The chair went over with a bang, dumping him onto the stage. Sarabeth jumped to help him up, but Nathan popped up before she got there. He was blushing. "Sorry!" he said. "Sorry. Sorry." He sat down again, glancing nervously around.

"It's okay," Maddie said. "No problem." She glared at Duncan, who was snickering. "What I was saying was that, Nathan, you need to think about Sam being an artist, and what that might mean about the way he carries himself." Then Maddie jumped up. "That reminds me!" she said. She rummaged around in her big blue plastic box. "Here are some lists for you all to take home. These are all the things we'll need for costumes, and I'm hoping that some of you will be able to find things in your attic, or at thrift stores. I'm most interested right now in shoes."

"Shoes?" Mel asked, looking skeptical. "Why shoes?"

"I like to ask my actors to start right out wearing the shoes they'll wear onstage," Maddie answered. "I believe it helps them focus on their characters. Plus, they get used to weird footwear!" She grinned. "Once I had to wear spike heels to play a 'doll' in *Guys and Dolls*. It took me *ages* to learn how to walk in those torture devices!" She giggled. "Okay. That's it. Let's get going, or we'll never get through the whole script! Everybody ready?"

Everybody nodded.

"All right, then. Sarabeth, you'll start us off!"

Sarabeth looked down at her script. "'Hello, Sam,'" she read. "'I didn't know *you'd* be here.'"

There was a silence.

Nathan fumbled with his script, turning pages back and forth.

"Act One, Scene One," Maddie said gently. "We're at the football game."

"Right. Right," said Nathan. He found the page, took a deep breath, and read, "'I only came because I knew *you'd* be here. I was never that interested in football.'"

"Great," said Maddie, folding her arms and leaning back in her chair. "Go on!"

"'Why, Sam Prescott!'" Sarabeth read. "'Are you —'"

But before she could finish her line, the lights went out.

All of them.

Suddenly, the auditorium was pitch black.

Chapter Nine

"Sal?" Maddie yelled.

"Working on it!" Sal yelled back. "Gotta find a flashlight first!"

"Everybody, stay where you are," Maddie said. "I don't want anyone tripping or falling off the stage."

In a few seconds, we saw the beam of a flashlight in the wings. I heard TJ asking Sal where the fuse box was. "Over here," Sal said, and the flashlight beam moved.

A few minutes later, I heard TJ's voice again. "Bummer!" he said. "It's locked."

"We won't be able to get into that today. Janitor's already gone." That was Travis's voice. He must have gone over to Sal and TJ to help. "Hey, what's this?"

"A note." That was Sal. His voice was flat.

"Sal?" Maddie called. "Can you bring that flashlight over here and lead us out of the auditorium?"

In a few moments, we were all gathered out in the hall. Sal showed us the note that had been attached to the locked fuse box. In that same, scrawled red writing it said,

It took me a second to make sense of it, because the writing was a little strange. The S's looked more like fives. But the overall intent was clear. It was minatory[13]. And it was creepy.

I saw Maddie glance at Sal. He shrugged. "Are you sure we can't get into the fuse box?" she asked Travis.

"Mr. Wilson has the only other key," he reported. "He's gone, too, right?" He turned to TJ. "I saw you coming out of his room a little while ago. Was he still there then?"

TJ shook his head. "He was gone. The room was open, so I got the hammer Sal sent me for, but I didn't see Mr. Wilson."

"Look," said Maddie. "We could use one of the classrooms and finish the read-through. But I think it might be better if we stop now. It's almost time for the late bus, anyway. Let's call it a day."

[13]minatory: threatening

Chapter Ten

"We'll go right on with our scheduled plans," Maddie said when we'd gathered in the auditorium the next afternoon. Sam and the tech people were already backstage, unrolling canvas and laying out wood for new flats. "We can't afford to miss a day. So we'll do rough blocking today, as planned. That means you actors will be moving around on the stage as you read from your scripts. I'll be telling you where to stand and when to move. Our stage managers will be taking notes so that one script will have all the directions. But you should each make your own notes, on your own scripts, as well."

She'd already announced that she had reported the threatening note to the administration and that her strategy was the same as before: Treat it as a prank, ignore it, and move on. That was fine with me. I can't deny that the note scared me a little, but I wanted to get going with this play.

Ashleigh and I took seats near Maddie in the auditorium. Nathan and Sarabeth and the other actors in the football game scene were onstage.

"Where's Mel?" Ashleigh whispered to me. She

was going over a cast list, sort of taking attendance.

I shrugged.

Just then, Mel dashed in, carrying a huge trash bag over her shoulder. A man who looked just like her (minus the blue fingernails) came in behind her, carrying another one. "Costumes!" Mel announced. "Sorry I'm late. This is my dad."

"We'll let it go, this once," Maddie said. "Especially if you brought shoes." She smiled at the man. "Nice to meet you," she added.

"We brought tons of shoes!" Mel's dad said. He opened his bag and reached in. "Old-fashioned sneakers for Sam," he said, pulling out a pair, "and saddle shoes for Donna —"

"Cool!" said Sarabeth from the stage. "Can I try them on?"

"Why don't you wait until our first break?" asked Maddie. "We need to move along if we're going to get enough done today."

While Maddie started rehearsal, Mel's dad unpacked the rest of the shoes and set them out for later. Meanwhile, I was watching Ashleigh closely as she took notes on everything Maddie told the actors.

"I want Donna down right, and Sam down left when the curtain goes up," Maddie said. "The people who are making up the football game crowd will be upstage."

Ashleigh was making a little diagram. "This'll tell us how it starts out," she whispered as she drew little boxes, labeling them with initials.

"Now, Donna, you'll turn to face left to look at Sam. On your line, you'll take a step forward. And Sam — I mean Nathan, but you all better get used to me calling you by your characters' names — on *your* line, you'll cross to Donna."

Ashleigh scribbled *step forward* near Donna's line, and *XR* next to Sam's. "Cross right," she explained, pointing to it.

"Got it," I said, making the same note in my own script. I was using a purple marker, figuring it would show up well. "And XL means cross left?"

"See?" she asked. "Told you it's easy. Listen, I have a dance rehearsal. So you can take it from here, right?" I gaped at her. She patted my shoulder and handed me her stage manager's notebook and a pencil. "Ditch the pen. Things always change. You'll do fine." Then she picked up her backpack and left. Maddie, busy with the actors, didn't seem to notice.

I scribbled away madly as she gave directions, not sure what I should or shouldn't be taking down. "*XL*," I wrote. "*Looks away.*" "*Touches hair.*" I crossed out lines when Maddie said we'd have to cut the scene shorter, added words when she said a line needed more explanation.

Finally, after what seemed like hours, she called a break. I blew out a breath and leaned back in my chair, shaking out my wrist to get rid of my writers' cramp. I looked over what I'd done so far, erased some of the sloppier notes, and rewrote them more carefully. Then I got up to stretch.

"Five minutes," Maddie said to me. "Hey, where's Ashleigh?"

"She had to go," I told Maddie. "Dance —"

She held up a hand. "Explain later. Right now it's your job to round up the actors. Tell them they have five" — she glanced at her watch — "no, *four* minutes." Obviously, she felt like Ashleigh and I were totally fungible[14] as stage managers.

I went out into the hall. "Four minutes!" I called to the kids who were out there, hanging around by the water fountain.

"Thank you," Sarabeth called back.

I looked at her, surprised.

"Theater tradition," she explained. "Stage manager tells us 'five minutes,' or 'places,' and we say 'thank you' so she knows we heard."

---

[14]fungible: interchangeable

"Cool," I said. "Thanks." I turned to go back inside, and she followed me, with Travis following *her.*

"I can't wait to try on these shoes," she said. She headed straight for the saddle shoes Mel had lined up with the others, sat down, and pulled on one. "Fits perfectly!" she said. She pulled on the other one — and shrieked.

"Ouch!" she cried. "What's this?" She pulled the shoe off again, looked inside, and pulled something out. Travis held out a hand and she gave it to him.

"A tack!" he said. "Jeez! Who would do *that*?" He looked disgusted. "Are you okay, babe?" he asked Sarabeth. "Did it cut you?"

She took off her sock and checked her foot. "I don't think so," she said.

Maddie turned to me. "Sounds like she'll live. We'll check the other shoes. Meanwhile, call 'places.'"

"Places!" I yelled. I was already getting into this stage manager thing.

The actors filed up onstage and returned to where they'd been before the break. Maddie had them reread a few pages in the script, just to get back into the feel of the play.

"Now, Sam, remember. You're seeing Sarabeth

in a whole new way. Suddenly, you realize she might like you, too," Maddie was saying, a few minutes later.

Nathan gulped. I could see it all the way from my seat. But before he could say his next line, the fire alarm went off.

"Arrgh!" Maddie cried. "I don't believe this!"

Everybody knew what to do. We've had plenty of fire drills. You don't hesitate when that alarm goes off. We all got up to file out of the auditorium. I grabbed my script — already precious to me because of all those notes I'd taken — and led the line up the aisle.

That's why I was the first to see the note. The one that had been taped to the main exit.

QUIT NOW OR IT'S CURTAINS FOR YOU!

Same red scrawl. Same weird S's. I took the note down and carried it outside to show Maddie.

When we were all gathered near the side exit of the school, Maddie looked it over. "Okay, that's it," she said. "I'm calling off rehearsal for the day again. Can everybody get a ride home?"

We all nodded. I looked over at Emma and she mimed holding a phone. Her mom's always willing to give us a ride. I took advantage of the kippage[15] around me to slip the note into my pocket. I

[15]kippage: excitement, confusion

wanted to take a better look at it later, under calmer circumstances.

Maddie and Sal lent out their cell phones. Ten minutes later, when Emma's mom pulled up, we were still hanging around outside. Good thing it wasn't too cold that day. We're not allowed to go back into the building until the firefighters have come and checked everything out. It was pretty obvious that someone had pulled the alarm as another stupid prank, but Maddie said rules were rules.

Emma's mom got out of the car. "You guys okay?" she asked.

Sal stepped forward. "They're fine," he said.

She looked at him. "Okay, good," she said. "That's good. I mean, I wouldn't want anybody to have gotten hurt or anything. So that's good." She seemed a little nervous. Maybe the fire drill made her worry about Emma. She's kind of a worrier.

"Can we give TJ a ride, too?" Emma asked. Katherine had already arranged a ride with Duncan. He's a junior and has his license.

"Sure," her mom said. "Of course."

"No, no, that's okay," TJ said. "I'll walk. I like to walk."

Emma and I climbed into her mom's car. I always like getting a ride from Emma's mom: She has the coolest car of any of my friends' parents. It's a lime-green new Bug. I don't know if you've ever ridden in one, but it's a lot of fun. Did you know Bugs even come with a little flower vase that attaches to the windshield? Emma's mom, Diana, always has a flower in hers. In the winter it's usually a fake one, but still. It makes the car special. That day's flower was a white silk rose. Very classy.

"I like your flower, " I said as we drove off.

"Thanks, Ophelia." She smiled at me in the rearview mirror. "So, what was that fire alarm all about?"

"Nothing," Emma said quickly. "Just a false alarm, I guess."

I knew enough to keep quiet. If Emma's mom knew about the threatening notes, she might not let Emma work on the play. Emma's an only child, and her parents tend to be a little overprotective. Lately, according to Emma, Diana and Emma's dad have been fighting about Emma's curfew, her activities — actually, they've been fighting a lot in general. Which makes Emma nervous, because she remembers how our friend Amanda's parents fought all the time just before they got divorced. But I thought Emma was worried over nothing. Parents argue sometimes — mine sure do — but it doesn't always mean the end of the world. And

Diana seemed like her normal self to me, only maybe a little nervous or distracted or something.

"That man with the red beard," she said now. "Is he helping on the play?"

Emma was playing with the radio dial, trying to find a decent station. "That's Sal," she said. "He's in charge of all the backstage stuff. He's nice."

"At first I thought he might be Maddie's, you know, boyfriend or something," I offered. "But I'm not so sure about that."

Diana just nodded.

"Hey, Mom," said Emma. "Can Ophelia and I go to the store for a soda? You can drop us there and I'll walk home after." She twisted around in her seat to look at me. "Want to?" she asked. She wiggled her eyebrows in this way that meant *say yes!*

"Definitely." I was dying to talk about the notes and the pranks. There was no way we could do that in the car.

"It's fine with me," said Emma's mom. "Just don't eat too much junk, and be home by six for dinner." She put on her turn signal as we passed the green and made a right onto East Street. Then, about half a block down, she pulled over to let us out. "You kids are so lucky to have this place," she said, looking over at the store. "I wish we'd had somewhere like this to hang out when I was your age. There was *nothing* to do after school back then. We used to say we lived in Cloverdull."

Cloverdale is a small town in a pretty little valley, with houses and businesses spread out along the main road (Route 20, which goes into Burlington, where Olivia lives) and up into the hills. The center of town is the village green. My house is on the west side of the green, on Spring Street. Route 20 runs along the north side. The Nguyens' general store is on the east side. So when I got out of the car, I could look across the green and see my house.

"Thanks for the ride!" I said to Diana.

"See you later," Emma said, coming around to the driver's side to kiss her mom.

Diana putted off and we turned to cross the street and go into the store.

The Nguyens opened this place just a few months ago. Before that, the only place to hang out or buy candy was the mini-mall out on Route 20. There was always a store on East Street, but for as long as I could remember it was closed and boarded up. Now the Nguyens' store is *the* place to hang out. They have a woodstove running all the time, so it's cozy and warm. They have a deli counter, a huge selection of penny candy, a well-stocked magazine and comic-book rack, and, best of all, a soda fountain with those old-fashioned stools you can spin around on.

"Hi, Mrs. Nguyen!" I called as we came in.

She smiled and nodded. "Hello, Ophelia. How are you, Emma?" The Nguyens came here from Vietnam, but they've had no trouble fitting into the community. They're really friendly and nice.

I waved to Mai and Tam, the Nguyens' little daughter and son. As usual, they shrieked and ran, smiling, to hide behind their mother. They are so shy!

Emma and I headed back to the soda fountain and sat down on the two stools at the end, our favorite spot. We ordered Italian sodas from Mimi, Mrs. Nguyen's sister, who works for them. I got peach-cranberry, my special invention, and Emma got hazelnut. Italian sodas are made with these delicious syrups that come in a million flavors. To make them, they pour a little of the syrup over ice and then fill it up with sparkling water. It's the best!

I took a long sip of my bright pink soda. "Ahh," I said. "Yum. Tastes like summer."

Emma sipped hers. "Yum," she echoed. "Tastes like — hazelnuts, I guess!" She giggled.

"Speaking of which," I said. "Isn't this nuts? The way somebody's trying to stop the play?"

Emma got serious. "I know," she said. "I'm wondering what they'll do next. I'm a little scared, to tell you the truth."

"Forget scared," I told her, even though I was frightened, too. "We have to do something."

"Like what?" She twirled the paper from her straw.

"Figure out who's doing it." I had decided that as soon as I saw the third note. Maddie might have been right to ignore the person pulling the pranks at first. But that plan wasn't working. Something else had to be done. And I was ready to do it.

"Us?" Emma asked.

"Sure," I said. "It wouldn't be the first mystery we've solved."

Emma considered that. "Okay. So, where do we start?"

I pulled a notebook out of my backpack. It happened to be the stage manager notebook that Ashleigh had dumped on my lap. I went to the back and flipped to a blank piece of paper. "We make a list," I told her. "Of things that have happened and of who could have done them." I took out my purple pen. INVESTIGATION I wrote across the top. Then I made two columns: EVENTS and SUSPECTS.

Emma pointed to the EVENTS column. "The first

thing was when somebody destroyed the cast list," she said. "With that green paint. And there was a note on it, in red."

I wrote it down. "Cast list destroyed," I said out loud as I wrote. "Green paint. Note in red." I paused. "What did it say, again?"

"'Break a leg,'" Emma answered.

"Oh, right!" I wrote that down. "Next was when the lights went out, right?"

She nodded. "And there was a note then, too. 'The show must not go on,' it said."

"Good memory." I scribbled some more. "Did you notice the weird S's in that note?" I asked her.

"Weird S's?" She shook her head. "Not really."

"I'll show you," I said. I pulled the third note out of my pocket. "Here's the one from today. It has weird S's, too."

"Ophelia!" she gasped. "You took it?"

"So?" I asked.

She just shook her head. "What if the police want to see it?"

"Then the police can ask their sister," I answered. Actually, it wouldn't be a bad idea to show it to Miranda. "Anyway, look at the S's."

"They *are* a little weird." Emma peered at the note.

"I wish there was a way to get handwriting samples from everybody," I said, tapping my pen on my front teeth. Then I thought of something. "Oh! Oh, oh, *oh*!"

"What?" Emma jumped a little when I yelled.

"Are you okay?" asked Mimi, rushing over.

"I'm fine," I said, waving a hand. "Sorry." I turned to Emma. "I just remembered. I have this notebook! And all the audition sheets are in here." I fumbled through the notebook until I found a pocket that held a thick sheaf of papers. "Check it out!" I crowed. "Handwriting samples from everybody involved in the play."

We quit making our list and started flipping through the audition sheets. I almost knocked over my soda, I was so excited. Maybe we were going to solve this case right now!

A few minutes later, we looked at each other and shook our heads. "Nothing," I said.

"Nothing," Emma agreed.

"Somebody's disguising their handwriting," I said, disgusted. "Either on the notes or on their audition sheet."

"Oh, well," said Emma. "Maybe that would have been too easy."

"Nothing wrong with easy," I told her. "But we'll figure it out. It's just going to take a little more work." I shuffled through the pile of papers on the counter until I found the list we'd been working on. "Back to the list." I added *tack in Sara-beth's shoe* under events. Then I finished that list off with *fire alarm pulled*.

"Good," said Emma. "I almost forgot about the tack. But that was a definite prank."

I looked over the list. "So, whoever did these things has some green spray paint and a red pen. They know their way around the theater. And they've been around over the last few days."

"And they're not afraid to pull a fire alarm," Emma added.

"The big thing is, what's their motive?" I asked. "I mean, why would somebody want to shut down the play?" I took a sip of my soda. "Like, what about Nathan, for example?"

"Nathan?" Emma looked confused.

"Sure," I said. "He's so shy. It's obvious that he's pushing himself to do this play. But maybe there's some deep psychological thing where he's really hoping he won't have to. I saw a thing like that on TV a while ago. It was like the guy's subconscious was making him commit crimes."

Emma looked skeptical. I wrote Nathan's name down anyway, under SUSPECTS.

"Who else?" I glanced down at the audition sheets. "Mel!" I said.

"Oh, come on!" Emma looked exasperated. "Why would *Mel* do those things?"

"I saw her face when she first read the cast list," I said. "She was *not* happy about being an understudy. Maybe she was trying to get back at Sarabeth, putting that tack in her shoe. And" — I got excited again. "Did you see her nail polish? It's, like, practically the same color as the paint on the list that day."

"She wears *green* nail polish?" Emma's not always as observant as I am.

"Well, blue," I said. "But metallic, just like the green. I bet she has a whole lineup of dark, metallic colors."

"Okay," said Emma. "Put her on the list. But I think you're nuts."

"So, who do *you* suspect?" I asked.

She thought for a minute. "Duncan?" she asked.

"Why Duncan?"

She shrugged. "Same motive as Mel, I guess. He's not happy with being an understudy."

I shook my head. "I don't think Duncan's the type," I said. "I just can't see him putting a tack in somebody's shoe."

I wrote his name down anyway. Sometimes the most unlikely suspect turns out to be the criminal, in the mysteries I've read.

"There's another one, too," Emma said.

"Another suspect?" I asked.

She nodded. "TJ." She looked down at her soda. "I know you like him, but —"

I held up a hand. "Wait. Like him?" I asked. "You mean, *like* him, like him?"

She gave me a little smile. "Don't you?"

"No! I mean — no!" All of a sudden, I realized something. The truth was, maybe I *did* like him. Just a little. I mean, I still barely knew him. But there was something about him. Something that made him different from all the guys I grew up with. His piano playing, his soft spot for cats . . . "He likes Katherine, anyway. He's always watching her. And I think that's why he came over the other night. So he could be around her. Anyway, why do you suspect him?" It was *definitely* time to change the subject.

"Well," Emma said, "he's handy with electricity, we know that. He's been around the whole time. And remember that day when the list was destroyed? We saw him practically running in the opposite direction."

I *did* remember. But it didn't mean anything. Did it? Suddenly, I had an image of TJ dropping that handful of silverware when he saw Miranda in uniform. But I didn't mention that to Emma.

"Also," Emma went on, "we don't know *anything* about him. I mean, he could have a criminal *record* for all we know."

I shook my head. "Em," I said. "I get what you're saying. And I'll write down his name. But I'll bet you he's the first person we clear. Whatever TJ is, he's no criminal."

I hoped I sounded a lot more sure than I felt.

Chapter Eleven

"I totally agree with Emma," said Katherine, later that night. "That TJ is a suspicious character, if you ask me. I mean, he never gives a straight answer about anything. Did you notice how he acted at dinner, when you asked him what those initials stand for?"

"What are you talking about?" I was in Katherine's room, watching her braid her hair in about twenty gazillion tiny braids. She sleeps with the braids in, then takes them out in the morning. Her hair looks awesome, all crinkly around her face, like angel hair. I've always wondered how my frizzy hair would look if I did that, but I don't have the patience to make all those braids.

Anyway, I'd gone into Katherine's room to tell her about the investigation Emma and I had begun. We'd decided it would be good to get Katherine in on it, too, so we'd have an extra pair of eyes.

Katherine sighed impatiently. "He took a huge mouthful of spaghetti, just so he wouldn't have to answer you. I saw it." She wrapped an elastic band around the bottom of a braid and started another.

"So?" I asked. "Maybe he just doesn't like to tell

his real name. That's his choice." For some reason, it was starting to bug me that everybody seemed to think TJ was some kind of juvenile delinquent.

"Whatever." Katherine shrugged. "I'd keep an eye on the guy."

Hmph, I thought. *He's sure keeping an eye on you.*

"We have to keep an eye on everybody," was all I said out loud. "We can't let this person stop the play."

Katherine held out a hand. "Hair band?" she asked. I handed her one.

"Have you started learning your lines?" I asked.

She just grinned. "'Mother, I have decided to marry Sam,'" she quoted. "'He'll be a famous artist someday, I just know it.'"

"Not bad!" I said. "If you ever want help, I'll read lines with you."

Katherine made a face at herself in the mirror. "I could take the whole thing more seriously if Travis were playing Sam instead of that nerdy Nathan," she said.

"Katherine!" I was shocked. "Come on, give the guy a break. He's trying so hard. And really, he's excellent when he's acting. He's only shy when he's —"

"Himself!" Katherine finished.

"He's a suspect, you know," I said.

She laughed. "Nathan? Okay, if you say so. But

I'm betting on TJ. And I'm going to be watching him."

That night, I used Poppy's fax/copier to make a copy of the note I'd torn down. Good thing I did, because the next day before rehearsal, Maddie asked if I had it and I had to hand it over.

She made an announcement before we started that day's work. "I've told the administration about what's been happening," she said. "I didn't want to get them involved if I didn't have to, but pulling the fire alarm is a crime, not just a prank. Mr. McGeorge is concerned enough that he has notified the police."

That was news to me. I figured I'd be hearing from Miranda that night and I could get the scoop on what the police were going to do. I didn't like hearing that Mr. McGeorge was involved. He's the vice principal, and he's in charge of school discipline. He's always in the halls, "checking in" with us. He seems like this jolly guy, always joking around. But he means business. And if he got concerned enough, he might shut down the play. Then not only would the play not happen, but the person pulling the pranks would have won! What a disaster. Emma and Katherine and I were going to have to work hard on our investigation if we were going to figure out who was responsible before things got out of hand.

With that in mind, I started doing some questioning. Have you ever seen that old TV show *Columbo*? The detective on that show seems like a total loser. He always needs a shave, his overcoat is rumpled, and his hair looks like he just slept on it. He has a way of talking to suspects really casually, so they don't even realize they're being interrogated. He sets a trap because they think he's just a half-asleep, totally-out-of-it guy. In truth, his mind is working a mile a minute and he's always a step ahead of the criminal. It's so cool to watch him work.

I tried to work *Columbo*-style, so the suspects wouldn't even know they were under investigation. Whenever I ran across someone during rehearsal that afternoon, I managed to ask a few innocent-sounding questions. "So," I asked Duncan, for example, when I was handing out changes to the script. "Is this your pen?" I held out a red felt-tip I'd brought from home, just for this purpose. I thought maybe I'd see something in his face when he thought I had found the pen he wrote the notes with.

But he just shook his head. "Nope," he said. "I'm not a red pen kind of guy. Purple, maybe. Never red."

A little later, Nathan and I were going over some blocking he didn't understand while some other actors worked on a scene. "See, here you'll pick up the phone," I said, pointing to the blocking notes I'd made in my script. "Then you walk over to the window. It'll all seem clearer when we have props and sets next week." I glanced at him and decided to try the pen trick again. "By the way," I said, holding it up. "Is this yours?"

"N-nope," he said, shaking his head. He stared down at his script as if it were the first time he'd seen it.

I looked at the back of his head. Was he nervous? I mean, more nervous than usual? Hard to say. I scribbled a little note in the back of the stage manager's notebook, where I was keeping track of the investigation. I figured that notebook was basically mine; Ashleigh hadn't even bothered to show up for that day's rehearsal.

Finally, toward the end of the day, I ended up sitting next to Mel during a break. "You know," I told her, "I think you would have made a great Donna." I watched her face. Was she steaming because she hadn't gotten a lead role?

If she was, it didn't show. "Too bad you weren't the one doing the casting, then," she said lightly.

I tried another subject. "Hey, I love that fingernail polish," I told her, pointing to her blue nails.

"Thanks," she said. "I have lipstick that matches it, but my mom thinks it's too wild for school."

"Does that metallic kind come in other colors?" I asked. "Like, I don't know, green? I like green."

She shrugged. "Don't know. Probably." She grabbed her script. "Gotta go!"

Here's the problem: I'm not Columbo. By that time, he would have cracked the case. Me? I wasn't any closer than when I'd started. I wondered if Emma or Katherine might be having better luck.

Read-through was almost over and I was adding some final blocking notes to my script when TJ came up to me. "Hey," he said. "You know, your dad told me about this other lamp in your house that never works right. I think he said it was in the study? Anyway, I've been thinking about it and I think I figured out how to fix it. So —" He looked down at his shoes.

I got it. I'm not dense. He wanted to be invited over again. "You want to come over and show him?" I asked. I didn't mind, even if he *was* just making it up as an excuse to be around Katherine. It would give me a chance to observe him, maybe ask a few Columbo-questions.

"Oh — okay!" he said, as if the idea hadn't occurred to him. "Sure."

"You might change your mind when you hear what's for supper this time," I said. "How do you feel about meat loaf and Brussels sprouts?"

"Love 'em both." His eyes met mine, and suddenly I had the feeling I was blushing. I hoped it didn't show.

I smiled back, thinking to myself, *Do I like him? And also, Could Emma and Katherine be right?*

Chapter Twelve

Emma had a dance class to go to, and Katherine was getting a ride home from Duncan again, so TJ and I sat together on the late bus. This was my chance to do the Columbo thing with him, even though I really didn't think he was a suspect.

"So, how do you like Cloverdale so far?" I asked.

"It's not bad." He played with the strap on his backpack. "A little — *small*, I guess. I'm used to being closer to a big city."

"Seattle?"

"Yeah." He nodded. "My dad and I, we used to go to concerts and stuff. He's a piano player, too."

"There are good concerts in Burlington sometimes," I said, feeling a little defensive about my little town. "They even have operas and everything."

He didn't look convinced, but he didn't say anything.

"Where are you living, anyway?" I asked. "And how did you end up in Cloverdale, Vermont?"

"My mom transferred to Vermont," he said. "She's working at the hospital in Burlington."

"Is she a doctor?" I felt like I was asking too many questions, but so far he didn't seem to mind.

He smiled. "She's a brain surgeon. You know how everybody always says, 'Well, it's not *brain surgery*,' when they're talking about something that's not so hard to do? In her case, it *is* brain surgery. She's really smart."

"Cool," I said. I noticed that he hadn't told me yet where his family was living. Maybe he'd avoided that topic on purpose. Or maybe he just forgot I asked. I decided to move on. "Do you have any brothers and sisters?"

"One sister," he said. "She's a lot older, though. She's in college."

That led me to my next question. "How do you like school here?" I was impressed with how well the conversation was going. I'd already learned much more about TJ than Emma had during that interview game.

He shrugged. "It's okay. Except I'm stuck in this boring algebra class. I already learned all that stuff last year."

"Can't they tell that from your records? Seems like they would have put you in another class," I said. The bus went over a big bump just then, and TJ's backpack flew off his lap. He grabbed for it.

"Aren't we almost at our stop?" he asked when he'd wrestled it back onto his lap.

87

I looked out the window. "Almost. So, what about your records? Wouldn't they show that you already took that class?"

He was playing with his backpack strap again, avoiding my eyes. "Don't know," he said. "I — I don't think they have my records. I left my old school in kind of a hurry."

"Really?" I asked. "Why —"

Darn. Just then, the bus stopped at Spring Street. Our stop.

When we got off the bus and started walking up the street, TJ started asking *me* questions. Like, what was it like to grow up in Cloverdale. And how was it having so many sisters. And whether I would be interested in playing some duets for flute and piano.

He got me so off track that I never did find out why he left his old school in a hurry. But I didn't forget about it. In fact, after he left that night I made a note of it on the suspect list. I hated to even think about it, but that really did sound suspicious. I mean, who leaves their school in a hurry? And why? It seemed pretty obvious that TJ had been in some kind of trouble. And maybe he was making trouble again.

Chapter Thirteen

"Okay, people!" Maddie clapped her hands. "You're all doing beautifully. Let's take a break, and when we come back we'll pick up in Act Two, Scene Three."

Everybody piled their scripts on the table near the wings and took off. There was already a tradition around break time: All the actors headed for the soda machine near the gym, while all the backstage people tended to go outside for a breath of air. Sal loved to show off the perfectly restored 1957 Cadillac he always parked near the back entrance; he was totally into old cars and so were a lot of the kids on the backstage crew. Emma usually joined me at the water fountain; neither of us felt completely at home with either group.

It was the next afternoon, and rehearsal was going smoothly. No fire alarms. No lights going out. No pranks at all. Maybe just the *idea* of Mr. McGeorge and the police getting involved had been enough to scare off the person causing trouble.

I hadn't had a chance to talk to Miranda yet,

since she had been working the late shift the night before. I wondered if the police had taken any action at all yet. They hadn't come to rehearsal, I knew that. Everything seemed totally normal that day.

Sal and his crew had finished building two big flats, each the size of a whole classroom wall. They were freestanding and could be moved on and off the stage, with a lot of people helping. One was going to be painted to look like an art studio in New York, and one would be Donna's room. The crew was already starting to paint the backdrop, which showed a country landscape dotted with houses. It was supposed to look like the fictional town of Butterfield, and it would show through the windows of Donna's room. Emma was in charge of sketching out the scene, and she had done an awesome job. She'd even limned[16] distant fields with cows in them and a purplish mountain range in the far background. She is *such* a good artist.

There would also be a set of bleachers for the football game scene, and a couple of smaller flats that could suggest an art gallery if they were turned one way and a living room if they were turned around. The backstage crew was rounding

[16]limn: to draw or paint

up tables and chairs and couches so the sets would look furnished. I had already "spiked the set" — that is, put X's of masking tape on the floor to show where things would go.

"So?" Emma asked while we were getting a drink at the fountain. "Any more clues?"

"Nothing, really," I said. "Nathan seems calmer today. Mel's acting a little goofy, but that's nothing new. What about TJ?"

She shrugged. "I can't tell. He doesn't talk much to me. I'll tell you one thing, though. He and Sal really seem to get along. They have these long conversations about music. I don't even know what they're talking about."

Just then, Maddie stuck her head around the corner. "Can you round up everybody?" she asked me. She was used to the fact that Ashleigh was hardly showing up. I had kind of graduated to stage manager already. Which was a little scary, but also very cool. So far, I was on top of things.

"Come with me?" I asked Emma. We walked down the hall to where the actors were. "Five minutes!" I said.

"Thank you!" answered Sarabeth, as usual. She and Travis were sharing a soda, sitting a little apart from everyone else. She stood up to follow me back to the auditorium. But Travis grabbed her arm.

"Ow!" I heard her say. She frowned at him. "That hurt!"

"Oh, come on," he said, smiling up at her. "I barely touched you, Miss Sensitive. Here, let me kiss it and make it better." He made smooching noises on her elbow. "Anyway, what's your hurry? She *said* five minutes. Sit and finish your soda."

"I don't want any more," Sarabeth said, handing him the can. "And my hurry is that I promised to run a few lines with Nathan." She turned and walked away, so she didn't see the look on Travis's face.

But I did.

He looked hurt. But the look flashed over his face and disappeared in the space of two seconds. Then he shrugged, lifted the soda can, drank the rest of it down, and popped a perfect shot into the trash. "Two points!" I heard him say under his breath.

"Coming, Ophelia?"

I turned to see Maddie calling me from down the hall and realized that I'd sort of been in a daze, staring at Travis. It was easy to stare at him; he was just so good-looking. But it was embarrassing to be caught. Especially by Maddie! "Coming!" I called back.

Travis glanced at me and smiled. It was as if he knew I'd been watching him. He nodded to me.

"You're doing a great job," he said. "You're already a better stage manager than Ashleigh ever was."

Wow. Now I was *really* embarrassed. I couldn't believe Travis had even noticed me or had a clue about what I'd been doing. I blushed. "Thanks," I said. "I mean — thanks." I walked away, feeling like an idiot. A very happy idiot.

"Okay, people," Maddie said, clapping her hands for quiet when we were all reassembled. "Let's finish up this read-through. Remember, next week we go off book. This is your last rehearsal with scripts."

Everybody groaned. Nathan looked terrified. "Off book," I'd learned, means that the actors are supposed to have memorized their lines. So far, they were still carrying scripts, and either reading from them or at least checking them once in a while. Next week, they'd put them away and count on me to prompt them if they forgot a line. I had a feeling I was going to be pretty busy, following along with the script and prompting.

"Let's go back to the beginning of Act Two," Maddie said, "and try to run it."

"Run it" is another theater term I'd just learned. It means going straight through a scene, without stopping to discuss blocking, line delivery, gestures, "business," or any of the other things Maddie had been working on. "Business," to give you one last theater word, is the stuff that actors do while they're delivering a line. Making a cup of coffee, for example, or reacting to something. Or bending down to tie a shoe.

Speaking of tying a shoe, it was getting interesting to watch read-throughs, because the actors had started to wear parts of their costumes. Sarabeth was walking around in her saddle shoes, and Nathan had on vintage high-tops. Mel, as Donna's mother, wore a frilly white apron. Katherine had a pink mohair twin set: two matching sweaters, one a pullover with short sleeves and one a cardigan. It was perfect on her, and perfect for Veronica.

I wasn't the only one who thought read-throughs were getting interesting. I noticed that Sal seemed to be spending more and more time watching rehearsals from the wings, while his crew worked. I thought it was a little weird — but maybe he'd just always loved theater. After all, didn't he and Maddie meet when they were both working on a musical?

Katherine was standing stage right just then, near Nathan. Sarabeth and Mel were stage left. This scene had alternating moments between Veronica and Sam, in New York, and Donna and her mother, back in Butterfield.

"Okay, let's start at the top," said Maddie, taking the seat next to mine. She leaned over to whisper to me. "Keep an eye on Sarabeth here," she said. "I think she's having trouble remembering the blocking for this scene. We'll go over it later if she gets it wrong again."

I nodded. It was cool feeling like the assistant director.

Katherine looked down at her script. "'Sam, why do you always seem so distant?'" she read. "'It's like you forget I exist sometimes.'"

Nathan was gazing off to the left, where there would eventually be a wall and a window. "'I'm sorry,'" he read. "'I don't mean to hurt you. It's just that I can't stand that Pepto-Bismol sweater.'"

"What?" Katherine stared at him.

He looked down at the script again. "Th-that's not the line," he said.

"No kidding," said Katherine frostily.

Nathan looked out at me and Maddie. "Sorry."

"Go on," said Maddie. Nathan looked down at his script again. "'I mean, you look like a big hunk of bubble gum,'" he read. He stared at the script. "Wait —"

Katherine glared at him.

"Nathan, that's enough," said Maddie. "We don't have time for fooling around."

"But I'm not —"

"Let's move on to Donna's scene with her mom," said Maddie.

Sarabeth nodded. She looked down at her script. "'Oh, Mother, do you think he'll ever come back?'" she read. "'I miss Sam so much. I wish he hadn't joined the circus.'"

"Huh?" said Nathan from across the stage. "The circus?"

"What's going on here?" Maddie demanded. "Let's get back on script, everybody."

"But the scripts are ridiculous!" Sarabeth said. "Look at my next line! I start talking about how Sam has become a lion tamer!"

As I headed up onto the stage to look over Sarabeth's script, I had a sinking feeling. Another prank. Just when I thought everything was going so smoothly. I looked around. Who could be responsible? Sal's crew was working backstage. I saw TJ there, holding a paintbrush as he stepped back to look at the "kitchen wall" he was painting. Emma was next to him, and I saw her looking back at me. Obviously, she'd heard what was going on, and she was wondering the same thing I was. I met her eyes and shrugged. Sal was listening, too. He always seemed to be keeping a close eye on the actors. Now he seemed concerned.

Sarabeth handed me her script and pointed to the lines she'd been reading. "See?" she asked. "It's right there in black and white."

I looked down at the script. Sure enough, what

she'd said was written on the page. But something about that page looked different. The paper was a different shade of white and — I rubbed a page between my fingers — not as heavy as the paper in the rest of the script. Somebody had inserted new pages into everyone's scripts!

I looked around. All the usual people were there: Nathan, Sarabeth, Duncan . . . and Mel. Mel, who had a strange look on her face. I took a step closer, and saw something that clinched it.

A little white dot, sticking to her sweater.

A little white dot, like the ones that are left behind when you punch holes in paper so you can stick it in a notebook.

I reached out and plucked the dot off her shoulder. And I was about to confront her when she burst out laughing. I mean, she totally cracked up. She laughed and laughed, while the rest of us just stared at her. "Ha!" she said when she could finally catch her breath. "Gotcha!" She looked straight out at me. "*Some* people seem to think I'm responsible for those stupid pranks. Well, I'm not. But it sure is easy to mess things up if you want to!"

Maddie shook her head. "You changed the scripts?" she asked.

Mel nodded, still laughing. "It was easy. I did it during break, when everybody's scripts were in a pile in here. I just slipped in some new sheets that I typed up last night."

I saw a little smile on Maddie's face. She was mad, but she couldn't help herself. "Very amusing," she said. "And, Mel, your point is well taken. It's easy to disrupt a play. But let's not make a habit of it, okay? We have a tight schedule, and while I want us to have fun, we have to work, too."

Very amusing. Ha! I didn't think it was all that funny. And I wasn't completely convinced that Mel was innocent of the other crimes. But at least this one wasn't scary, like some of the notes we'd gotten. Maybe Mel's prank would be the last.

Chapter Fourteen

"'But Sam, I found this letter!'" Katherine, stage left, held up an envelope. "'I know all about Donna. You're still in love with her, aren't you? *Aren't* you?'"

Nathan paced around stage right. "'Oh, Veronica, can't you forget about it? Jealousy is a bitter, terrible emotion that does nobody any good. It'll eat you up inside, make you do things you'll regret.'"

Maddie looked over at me and nodded, eyebrows up. I nodded back. It was Monday afternoon, our first rehearsal off book, and the actors were doing a great job. I was following along in my script, checking to make sure they had the blocking right, standing by if they needed me to prompt. I'd had a few calls for "line!" (That's how actors ask for a prompt. They're supposed to avoid breaking out of their character any more than that.) But that was to be expected. The actors were just starting to learn their lines.

"I'm going to check the prop table," I whispered to Maddie. "I'm not sure the newspaper is on it." After the next couple of lines, Sam was going to go to the door and fetch the newspaper. I had forgotten to check with Kayla, the girl doing props, to make sure she'd brought one. We were trying to pull everything together now: props, blocking, and lines. The play was really starting to take shape, despite all the "distractions" we'd had. In fact, things were going so well that Emma and Katherine and I had pretty much put our investigation on the shelf. After all, if there weren't any more pranks, what was the point? Maybe the person had gotten it out of his or her system. Anyway, Emma was busy painting scenery, Katherine was busy learning her lines, and I was helping with both. On Saturday I'd spent the whole afternoon painting clouds on the backdrop, and on Sunday I'd "run lines" with Katherine for hours.

Carrying my notebook and script, I headed up to the right wing. Onstage, Nathan and Katherine went on with their scene. "'But Sam,'" Katherine pleaded, "'I know all about Donna' — wait! I already said that. Oops!" She looked around for me. "Line!" she called when she spotted me in the wings.

I had my finger marking the page in the script, so I found the line quickly. "'I know I shouldn't be —'" I began, giving Katherine a hint.

"'Jealous.'" She picked it right up. "'It's tearing me apart. And after all, you married *me*.'"

"'That's right,'" Nathan said. "'Try to remember that, darling.'" As he spoke, he crossed to the "door" (it wasn't actually there yet), pretended to open it, and reached out for the newspaper.

Fortunately, it was there. Kayla must have remembered without my telling her. Since I was standing right there, I picked it up from the prop table and handed it to him. He gave me a little nod as he took it. For a second, I thought he was going to drop it, the way he always dropped everything. But he was Sam, not Nathan. He didn't drop it. He just turned, closed the "door," and walked back toward Katherine.

He sat down in the "easy chair" (so far just a folding wooden chair) and opened the paper. "'Now, if we're done with this ridiculous conversation, I'd like to —'" He stopped in midline.

There was a moment of silence.

He didn't ask for his line, but I gave it to him anyway. "'Read my paper in peace,'" I said softly. I was still in the wings.

Nathan didn't seem to hear me. He was staring down at the newspaper.

"Nathan?" Maddie asked from the audience.

"That's it," he said, sounding stunned. "I quit."

"What's going on?" I walked toward him.

He didn't answer. He just turned the paper a little, so I could see it.

I gasped. Katherine came running. "What?" she asked.

She looked over our shoulders.

We were staring down at another note, scrawled in that familiar red handwriting. DON'T MAKE A SCENE — JUST TAKE A BOW AND EXIT NOW! it said. Above it, in that same green paint, was a crude drawing of those two theater masks like the ones on that sign I'd seen, the one that got me into this whole mess. I guess they stand for comedy and tragedy. But in this case, there was no comedy mask. One mask was frowning, like the usual tragedy mask. It even had a few tears falling from one eye. But the other was a mask of pure terror. It looked the way someone's face would look if they were seeing a horrible accident: eyes bugged out, mouth in a frightening grimace. It was downright scary.

By then, Maddie had joined us onstage. She stared down at the note and shook her head. "That's awful," she whispered. "But Nathan, you can't quit! We need you!"

"I don't care," he said. "I can't take it anymore. It's — it's hard enough without these notes." He threw down the paper and walked away, tripping over the chair as he exited, stage right.

Chapter Fifteen

"Notes?" Maddie asked. "You mean this isn't the first?"

Nathan was on his way to the door. He turned around for a second and shook his head. Then he left the auditorium, without looking back. The rest of us stared after him. There was a brief silence, and then there was a callithump[17] as everybody started talking at once.

Maddie held up her hand. "People! People!" she said. "Settle down!" I saw her glance over at Sal, as if she wanted to ask his advice. He was standing in the wings, looking worried. Maddie looked at me next. I met her glance and gave her a little nod. Whatever she wanted to do, I would be there to help.

She took a deep breath. "Look," she said, speaking loudly enough for everyone to hear. "Someone is trying to ruin this play, put a stop to it. I can't let that happen. But I also have your safety to think about. I am going to speak to Mr. McGeorge and

[17]callithump: hubbub

103

show him this note. I expect he'll be in touch with the police. Meanwhile, I want this rehearsal to continue. We don't have a day to waste. Opening night isn't far off, and we have a lot of work to do."

She looked around. "Duncan? Are you here?"

Duncan stepped forward.

"I want you to read Nathan's part," Maddie told him. "Can you do that?"

He nodded. "Sure. I even have some of it memorized. Isn't that what understudies are supposed to do?"

Maddie smiled at him distractedly. "Thank you, Duncan." She turned to me. "Ophelia, I'd like you to be in charge of rehearsal until I get back from talking to Mr. McGeorge. Start at the top of this scene and run as much of Act Two as you can."

I gulped. "Okay," I told her. "I can do that." I was trying to convince myself as much as Maddie, but she just nodded.

"I know you can." She reached for the newspaper Nathan had dropped. I reached down, too, and handed it to her. But not before I'd quickly torn off a little corner of the note, where the green paint was. I don't think Maddie noticed. She had already turned to address everyone again. "Please give Ophelia the same respect you would give me," she told the cast. "I'll be back as soon as I can." She handed me her director's script, turned, and glided offstage. I saw Sal reach out to pat her shoulder as she passed him.

I looked over at Emma. She and TJ were standing in the wings near Sal, watching me. Both of them gave me the thumbs-up.

Then I looked at Katherine. She just raised her eyebrows and one corner of her mouth, as if to say, "Show us what you can do."

I took a deep breath as I walked off the stage and took the seat Maddie usually sat in. Duncan had joined Katherine onstage. He was looking down at his script, his lips moving as he brushed up on his next lines. "Okay, everybody," I said. My voice came out all squeaky. I cleared my throat and tried again. "Okay," I said. "Places, everyone! Let's take it from the top of Act Two."

There was really nothing to it. I basically did the same thing I had been doing as stage manager: following along in the script, prompting actors when they needed lines, making notes on things they'd gotten wrong or things we might want to adjust next time around, such as the way Katherine slammed the door when she left at the end of the scene. I also noted that we'd need another newspaper.

Everything went pretty smoothly, except when Duncan made this comment to Sarabeth, something like "Guess I'll be kissing you now," and I practically had to hold Travis back from jumping up onstage to "teach him a lesson."

It seemed like I could handle this directing thing. What I *couldn't* do was also think about who might have been responsible for that nasty note. Poor Nathan! What kind of creep would pick on him? He was so nervous and overwhelmed already; it hadn't taken much to scare him off.

But as soon as Maddie reappeared in the seat next to me, my mind started working. I watched Duncan onstage. He looked pretty pleased with himself, strutting around in the lead role.

And what about Kayla? She'd had the best chance of messing around with one of the props. I added her name to the SUSPECTS list in the back of my notebook.

We were in the middle of Scene Four when Miranda arrived. "Hey," she whispered, slipping into a seat one row behind me. Then she introduced herself to Maddie. "I'm Miranda Parker," she said. "I'll be investigating this case. For today, I'd just like to observe for a little while, if that's all right with you. Eventually, I may have to question some of your cast and crew. Can I see the most recent note?"

Maddie handed it over, and Miranda examined it.

I turned to her. "I think we should try to find out

where the person got that paint," I whispered. "Maybe that will help narrow down the suspects."

She looked at me, raised her eyebrows, and nodded. "Good thinking," she said. "Want to come along while I look into it?"

"Go ahead," Maddie said. "We're almost done here, anyway."

We left about ten minutes later. I gave a little wave to Emma and Katherine as I walked with Miranda. I noticed TJ watching me leave, as well. I wondered if *he* was wondering what Miranda and I were up to.

Outside, I got into the squad car with Miranda. It was the first time I had ridden in it (Miranda only recently started driving patrols), and I had to admit it was pretty exciting. I looked everything over carefully, from the two-way radio to the button that activated the lights and sirens. There was a little part of me, the five-year-old part, that wished we could put the siren on, just for the short drive to town.

Our first stop was the Nguyens' store. Miranda had the note with her, for evidence, but I pulled out the little piece I'd torn off. "We don't need to be showing that note all over," I said. She agreed. I showed the color to Mr. Nguyen. "Do you carry this paint?" I asked.

He shook his head. "No, no," he said. "We only

have the basic paint. White, black, red. Nothing fancy like that." He scratched his head. "Maybe try the hardware store out on Route 20?"

That's where we went next. No luck. They had whole aisles of paint, but the manager said they didn't carry anything like the color we showed him. "Looks like auto paint to me," he said. "You know, for touching up scratches on cars? I'd try the Subaru dealer two doors down."

The parts manager at the Subaru place recognized the paint chip right away. "Sure, we can get this," he said.

"You don't have it in stock?" Miranda asked.

"Nope." He shook his head. "That's an old color. We'd have to order it special."

We tried a couple of other car dealerships, but nobody had the paint on hand.

Finally, Miranda drove me home. "Dead ends are a part of detective work," she said to me, shrugging. "But we'll keep trying. Meanwhile, keep an eye on those suspects." I'd shared my list with her.

"I will," I promised.

It wasn't until later that night, *way* later, that it came to me. I was in bed, nearly asleep, when I realized there was one other place we might find that paint. And it was only a few doors down from the very place we'd started out that day.

Mr. Wilson's shop.

Chapter Sixteen

The next day, I was dying to get into Mr. Wilson's shop to check on whether they had that paint on the shelf. I knew they worked on cars in there. Wouldn't it make sense that they had auto-body paint? But my day was so busy that I never got the chance. Finally, just after last bell, I made a run for the shop, hoping to get in there in the few minutes between last bell and the start of rehearsal.

I pulled on the door. Darn! It was locked. Mr. Wilson was already gone for the day.

Frustrated, I turned to leave — and saw Sarabeth, deep in conversation with Nathan, next to a nearby locker.

I didn't mean to eavesdrop. I know it's not right. But I must have a detective gene in my blood or something. I couldn't help myself. After all, as Miranda had pointed out the day before, Nathan was still a suspect. If my idea of his deep psychological need to ruin the play (and get out of being onstage) was right, he was actually a *prime* suspect. So I slowed down as I walked by, hoping to overhear what they were talking about.

"Nathan, please," Sarabeth was pleading. "You

have to come back. Duncan just doesn't understand the part the way you do. The play won't be any good without you."

Nathan fiddled with the lock on the locker. The back of his neck was the deepest red I'd seen yet. "Like I said yesterday," he finally said, "it's too hard. Just — too hard. Do you know what it's like to get notes like that? I threw them away and tried to forget about them. But I couldn't. Anyway, this whole acting thing — I don't know if I have what it takes."

Sarabeth put a hand on his shoulder. "I know you're pushing yourself, Nathan. I know it's hard. But sometimes we just have to do things, even if they're difficult." Suddenly, she looked very sad, and I noticed that her eyes were kind of squinchy and red, as if she'd been crying recently. "I just did something hard," she confessed.

Nathan glanced up at her questioningly.

She bit her lip. "I just broke up with Travis."

Chapter Seventeen

As if that wasn't enough of a shock, I had another one as soon as I entered the auditorium a few minutes later. There were only a few people there yet, but all of them were clustered in the wings, looking at something. I joined TJ and Emma, who were standing near Sal.

"What happened?" I asked, as if it weren't obvious. All three of them were staring at the backdrop, the one we'd already done so much work on. It was nearly ready to be hung up, or at least, it had been.

Now, it was nearly destroyed.

The second I looked at it, every thought I had about Sarabeth and Travis's breakup flew out of my head.

Someone had taken a sharp tool and slashed through the backdrop in a dozen places, creating huge gashes in the scene we'd painted. Emma's cows, my clouds, all of it — ruined. And, in a huge scrawl across the whole thing, someone had sprayed — in that same green paint — the words FINAL CURTAIN. SHOW'S OVER.

Emma was shaking her head. "How could somebody do this?" she asked. She looked as if she was in shock, and I didn't blame her. She'd done so much work on that backdrop!

I glanced at TJ, trying to gauge his reaction. Was he upset? Surprised? Or, maybe, *guilty*?

He just looked sad. And a little mad. "Maybe we can fix it," he said.

Sal frowned. "I don't know. It's pretty messed up."

"Can we try?" Emma asked. "I mean, maybe I could paint over the green paint. I don't know how we can fix the tears, though."

"What about taping them from the back?" TJ asked. "It won't be perfect, but maybe it doesn't have to be. As long as it looks okay from the audience, that's the main thing."

"We don't have much time to spend fixing it," Sal said. "We still have a bunch of other stuff to build and paint."

Just then I looked out into the auditorium and saw that Ashleigh was making one of her rare appearances. "Maybe I can help!" I said. I ran down to ask Ashleigh if she could cover the stage manager job that day.

"What else would I be here for?" she snapped, looking at me as if I were nuts. As if she'd been there all along, instead of sticking me with everything she was supposed to do.

"Right," I said. I didn't want to get into it with her. "There's been another prank. The backdrop's ruined. I'm going to help fix it." I shoved the stage manager notebook into her hands. "There are lots of new notes," I told her as I turned to head back to Sal, Emma, and TJ. "And I made a list of props for each scene. It's on the front page. Oh — and don't forget to remind Maddie about —"

"I can take it from here," Ashleigh interrupted.

Fine. Whatever. I headed back to Sal and the others.

When Maddie arrived, she looked over the damage and shook her head. Everybody was talking about the latest incident, but she cut them off. "Let's not give this person the satisfaction of ruining today's rehearsal," she said. "Sal has this in hand. We'll let Mr. McGeorge and the police know what happened. Meanwhile, let's get on with what we're here for." She looked more upset than I'd ever seen her — and disgusted, too. I liked it that she didn't seem beaten by these stupid pranks. They just seemed to make her more determined. She took one last look at the backdrop and shook her head. Then she clapped her hands. "All right, then," she said, turning away. "Actors, let's get to work. We're going to try to run the whole play today, from the beginning to the end. I'm not going to interrupt unless I absolutely have to." She glanced back at me, a question on her face. I nodded toward Ashleigh, who was already sitting in the audience, going over the script. "She's here, so I'm going to help with this," I said, gesturing toward the backdrop. Maddie smiled and nodded.

Just then, I saw Nathan walk into the auditorium. A few of the actors onstage spotted him, too, and started applauding. Maddie ran over and gave him a big hug. "Are you back to stay?" she asked. I couldn't hear his answer, but apparently it was the one she wanted, because she threw back her head and let out a happy whoop. I was glad to see him, too. Even though his reappearance pretty much took him off the suspect list. He wouldn't sabotage a play he *wanted* to be in, would he?

I couldn't help noticing that Duncan didn't seem quite as happy as everyone else. But he didn't look like a pernicious[18] maniac, either. I couldn't quite picture him ripping that backdrop to shreds. Anyway, why *would* he? If his motive had been to get rid of Nathan, he had succeeded. (For a little while, anyway.) But who *had* done it? If I didn't find out soon, it might be too late.

According to our schedule, next week would be our last week of rehearsals. We'd have a few run-

---

[18]pernicious: wicked, villainous

throughs just with the actors. Then we'd have a tech rehearsal with lights and sound effects. The day after that would be our dress rehearsal, and the day after *that* — if all went well — would be opening night.

I glanced around at the scenery and sets Sal and his crew were working on. Was there really time to get everything done, especially now that the biggest project had to be practically *re*done?

There had to be time. I did not want my first experience as a stage manager (or assistant stage manager, or whatever I was) to be a failure.

"Yo, Parker," TJ said, grinning at me. "Earth to Parker."

I realized everyone was waiting for me to help. We flipped the backdrop over, and, using several rolls of sticky silver duct tape (every Vermonter's favorite fix-it tool), we got to work patching up the horrible slashes. It felt good to work; it kept me from feeling as angry — or as scared — as I might have if I weren't busy.

While we worked, I kept half an ear on what was going on out on the stage. I'd heard every line of dialogue so many times by then that I could practically say the lines along with the actors. Apparently, somebody else had been paying attention, too.

115

TJ.

I looked up at one point to see him mouthing Sam's lines along with Nathan. "'But Donna,'" he said silently, with just the hint of a smile, "'you know I love you more than anything. I promise I'll come back.'"

"'Oh, Sam,'" I mouthed back, grinning at him, "'I know you will. And I promise I'll wait for you. I'll wait forever, if that's how long it takes.'" I clutched my heart dramatically.

"'Donna,'" TJ mouthed.

"'Sam,'" I mouthed back.

"Bull," said Sal, out loud.

I smiled at him. "I know, it's a little over-the-top, isn't it? But it's *so* romantic. I think the audience is going to eat it up."

"Romantic, maybe," Sal said. "But that's not exactly how it all happened."

"What?" I was so surprised I dropped the scissors I was using to cut tape.

"How do you know?" Emma asked.

Sal didn't answer right away. Then he sighed and bent to stick on another piece of tape. "I knew the playwright," he said finally.

We tried to ask him more questions, but he shushed us. "Let's concentrate on our work, okay?" he asked. "We've got too much to do to waste time talking."

116

Emma and I looked at each other. And we stopped asking questions. But as soon as we were done for the day, we headed straight for the library. It was time to find out a little more about a certain N. P. Ellison.

Chapter Eighteen

"Where do we even start?" Emma asked. We were in the reference room at the library, one of my favorite places in Cloverdale. I always like the feeling of being surrounded by facts. If you take all those books and add in the Internet, you should be able to learn about or figure out anything in the universe.

But sometimes you need a little help. And that's where Ms. Rosoff, the reference librarian, comes in. She and I get along really well. She lives just down the street from me, and I always see her out walking her dog, Misha. He's a malamute; he looks kind of like a big, friendly wolf with this beautifully fluffy, curly tail that he holds high over his back.

"Can I help you girls with something?" Ms. Rosoff asked just then. She'd come into the reference room to put a book away. "Hello, Ophelia. Hello, Emma."

"Hi, Ms. Rosoff," I said. "How's Misha?"

"Just as stubborn as ever," she said, winking at me. "What's up?"

"We're looking for some information about a local author," I said. "A playwright named N. P. Ellison." I had a feeling Maddie wanted the play to be a surprise for the town, so I didn't tell Ms. Rosoff why we were looking.

She just nodded. "I've heard of him. I think that's a pen name, though. Let's try the Vermont section," she said.

Of course. I should have thought of that. She led us into another room, where all the books about Vermont are kept. There are some beautiful photography books there, and also some really interesting history books. There's also a whole shelf full of books by Dorothy Canfield Fisher, who was a Vermont author. She wrote a book called *Understood Betsy*, about a city girl who comes to live in Vermont. It's one of my favorite books of all time.

"You'd probably find your author on this shelf," Ms. Rosoff said, pointing to a low shelf. "We have books, as well as some articles, original plays, and even an opera. Not all the authors are from Cloverdale, of course. But they're all from nearby." She turned to leave. "All set? I'd better get back to the desk."

"Thanks!" I said. I squatted down to look the shelf over. It didn't take long to find a big notebook with N. P. Ellison's name on the spine. Next to it were a couple of published plays, but I had a feeling any information about our play, which hadn't been published, would be in that notebook.

Emma and I sat down at a table and I started paging through the notebook. Sure enough, the first section was an exact copy of the script we were working on. "This must be where Maddie found our play," Emma said.

The notebook contained not only our version, but several earlier drafts of the play. It would have been interesting to read through them, but I was in too much of a hurry. I wanted to find out more.

I flipped through the pages, not sure of what I was looking for. "I wonder what Ms. Rosoff meant about his name being a pen name," I said, thinking out loud as I glanced through some old letters about the play.

"Just means it's not his real name," Emma said. "Like, Mark Twain's real name was Samuel Clemens."

"I know that," I said. "I mean, how did N. P. Ellison come up with that name? And what's his *real* name?" I pulled out a letter. "Wait a second," I said. "Wait a *second!*"

"What is it?" Emma asked.

"I don't think Maddie saw this letter," I said.

"Why? What does it say?"

"It says that the play *A Love Like Ours* is never supposed to be performed in Cloverdale, Vermont."

"It's not? Why? What do you mean?" Emma got up to read over my shoulder. After a few seconds, she burst out, "Oh, my God! It's a true story! About his brother!"

I read ahead. "I don't believe this!" It turned out that N. P. Ellison had found his brother's real billet-doux[19] in the attic of the house they shared. "Sam" must have gotten both sets of letters back when the romance ended. And then his brother stole them to write a play! "Sam" was furious when he found out and upset about the whole town eventually learning everything about his romantic life. He made his brother promise that the play could never be put on in town.

"Oops," said Emma, staring down at the letter. "Maybe we'd better let Maddie know about this."

"It's a little late, isn't it?" I asked. I was staring at the typed name at the bottom of the letter. N. P. Ellison. Why did those letters look familiar? Suddenly, I grabbed a pencil and a piece of scratch paper and started scribbling letters.

"What are you doing?" Emma asked.

"It's an anagram," I said. "I just know it. An ana-

[19]billet-doux: love letters

121

gram for his real name." Emma looked doubtful, but I scribbled some more.

Then, almost like magic, the letters came together and I had what I was looking for: the playwright's real name.

SPONELLI.

Chapter Nineteen

I shoved the paper over so Emma could see the name. "Sponelli?" she said. "That's Sal's last name!"

We stared at each other. My mind was spinning. "So, wait. What does this mean? Is N. P. Ellison really dead? Is Sal actually a playwright?"

"Or —" began Emma.

"Oh, my God!" I said, realizing what she was about to say. "Sal could be the brother!"

"That would explain a lot," Emma said.

I thought about it. She was right. It *would* explain a lot. Like why Sal acted so weird when Maddie announced what play we were doing. And how he knew that the lines in the play weren't completely accurate.

And maybe, why he was so against the play being performed.

So against it that he would try to keep it from happening.

I nodded. Emma was nodding, too. "But — I *like* Sal," I said. "He seems like such a good guy." Then I pictured Sal standing proudly next to his old

Cadillac. A guy who restored cars would definitely have access to that special paint! I gulped.

"I know," Emma agreed. "Look, let's make sure we're right, first of all. Let's see if we can find an obituary for N. P. Ellison, or Mr. Sponelli, or whatever his name is."

We've looked up obituaries before at the library, when we were solving other mysteries. It's not so hard, once you know how to do it. It didn't take long to find an obituary for Victor Sponelli, also known by the *nom de plume*[20] of N. P. Ellison. Just as Maddie had told us, he had died young; he was only thirty-five when he was killed in a motorcycle accident, right at the crossroads of Route 20 and the Baileyville Road. I've passed by there a million times on my way to Burlington.

"How sad," said Emma, looking at his picture. He looked a lot like Sal, only slimmer and, naturally, younger.

" 'Survived by his parents, Mr. and Mrs. Ray Sponelli, and by his younger brother, Sal Sponelli,' " I read. "That's it, then. Sal is his only brother. That means — that means *Sal* is *Sam*!" No wonder he'd always seemed so interested in the dialogue onstage during rehearsals.

---

[20]*nom de plume:* French for pen name; also known as a pseudonym

"Wow," Emma said. We stared at the picture some more.

Just then, Ms. Rosoff passed by. "Finding what you need, girls?" she asked. She looked over our shoulders. "Victor Sponelli," she said. "I've heard of him. He had quite a reputation. When I went to Cloverdale High, you still heard his name. He was brilliant, supposedly. But also kind of, *you* know, a rebel."

"What about his brother, Sal?" I asked. "Know anything about him?" I'd forgotten that Ms. Rosoff grew up in town. She can come up with some pretty interesting information sometimes.

She shook her head. "Not so much," she said. "I think he left town when he was fairly young. He wanted to be a musician or something."

Emma and I shared a look. Just like in the play! I remembered Maddie saying that Sal had gone to Boston to try to be a musician. It was all fitting together.

"I bet you could find pictures of both of them in the old yearbooks we keep here," she said. "They're back in the Vermont section, where you were before."

"Great idea!" I said. "Thanks!" Emma and I practically sprinted back to the Vermont section. "Let's see," I said, doing some math. "Victor died when he was thirty-five, about ten years ago. And Sal was younger. Probably, like two years younger? So Sal's around forty-one, forty-two? Which means he would have graduated in . . ." I grabbed a year-book off the shelf. "I'll try this one."

"I'll try the year before," Emma said, taking another one.

We sat down at the table and started flipping through the pages. I checked for Sponellis in each year: freshman, sophomore, junior, senior. "Wow," I couldn't help saying. "Nice hairdos, huh?"

Emma laughed. "I know. And their clothes! It's all so seventies."

"Guess why?" I asked. This wasn't retro. This was real. People really did used to dress and do their hair that way. The boys had long bangs and the older ones had sideburns. The girls had *Charlie's Angels* hair, cut in shaggy layers.

"Nothing in this one," I said, putting it back and taking another. I was paging through it when I realized that Emma had stopped giggling. In fact, she had gone completely silent. I looked over and saw that she was staring down at a picture.

I went over to see what she'd found. "Whoa," I said. "Check out the prom king and queen." The guy was wearing what had to be a powder-blue tux. I could tell, even though the picture was black-and-white. He looked sort of familiar. "Hey!"

I said. "That's Sal!" I peered a little more carefully. The girl with him was wearing a long, satiny gown. She was petite, pretty. Her dark hair was long and straight and parted in the middle. She looked sort of familiar, too. "Where do I know her from?" I asked.

Emma turned to face me. Her eyes were huge, and she looked as if she was about to cry.

"Em?" I asked. "What's the matter?"

"Don't you get it?" she asked. "That's my mom."

Chapter Twenty

"Ophelia? *Ophelia!*"

Finally, I realized that someone was calling me. It was the next afternoon, at rehearsal. I was sitting at a little table in the left wing, the table that would become my command station during performances. I'd have a little light there, and room for my notebook and script, and a phone for emergencies, and a clock, and a flashlight, and . . . Anyway, I would have everything I needed to be on top of things. Ashleigh had already let me know that she'd only be covering one of the performances, and that I'd be responsible for the rest. That meant I'd be telling the house manager when to raise the curtain. Making sure the lighting crew followed their cues. Rounding up cast members when it was time for them to be onstage. Checking props. Prompting people if they blanked on their lines.

The list was endless. And I was nervous about it. But, at the same time, I knew that if I was organized enough I could do it. The problem was, I was having trouble focusing.

For example, just at that moment I was staring at Sal, who was working on the backdrop we'd fixed up. It looked surprisingly okay. You could hardly see the damage, and Emma was doing a great repainting job. We had covered the green marks with some special paint that hides darker colors, and now she and TJ were repainting the clouds and cows, while Sal filled in the meadow part of the landscape. Travis had come to help, too. (I think maybe he'd really come mostly so he could try to talk to Sarabeth, but it was nice of him to pitch in.)

Anyway, I was staring at Sal. How could I not? Suddenly, I knew that Sal was Sam and Diana Stone was Donna. I'd never be able to look at either of them the same way again.

As for Emma, she was pretty freaked out. I couldn't blame her. How would *you* feel if you suddenly realized that this guy you'd come to know and like was actually your mom's first love?

After all, we didn't really know what finally happened between "Sam" and "Donna." The play ended on a very ambiguous[21] note. It didn't help that Emma was already worried about how much her parents were fighting lately. What if part of Diana was still in love with Sal?

On top of that, we had to deal with the very real possibility that it was Sal who was sabotaging the

[21]ambiguous: not spelled out or definite

play. It was understandable that he wouldn't want it performed in town, where lots of people would know who Sam and Donna really were. But would Sal really pull pranks like destroying the very scenery he was working so hard to build? It was hard to imagine.

Of course, it was also hard to imagine Sal and Diana as high-school sweethearts, but facts were facts.

So. I was staring at him. I didn't hear my name at first. Finally, I realized someone was calling me. I turned to see Maddie standing there, giving me a funny look. "Ophelia, are you ready to start?" she asked. "Ashleigh isn't here today, so I'll need you to prompt the actors with lines and blocking."

I nodded. "Oh, sure," I said. "I'm here!" I tried to sound capable and efficient, instead of like the airhead I must have resembled. "How about if I work from this table today, since this is where I'll be during performances?"

"Great," she said. "Are you sure you're not too squeezed in?"

There were big flats on either side of me, scenery built by Sal and his crew. Both were built out of Masonite, with wooden frames. They stood up-right because of the special wooden triangle bases the crew had attached at the bottom. The one in front of me was supposed to be a kitchen wall and window, and the one in back of me was the art gallery scene, showing a white wall hung with Sam's paintings. The crew had done a fantastic job. TJ and Emma had actually signed the paintings they'd done, in tiny letters nobody would ever see. TJ's was of a stylized landscape, and Emma's was a portrait of a girl and her dog.

"Sure, I'm fine," I told Maddie. My spot was a little cramped, but it didn't matter. I could see the stage well, and during performances the flats would be in another place so I'd have more room.

"Call five minutes, then," she said, waving as she walked down to take her seat.

I got up and strolled around the theater and the hallways nearby, calling, "Five minutes, everybody!"

It felt good to hear Nathan's voice join Sarabeth's, saying, "Thank you!" From what I'd heard, he was really happy to be back. That *did* kind of bump him off the suspect list. I'd also heard that Duncan, instead of being disappointed, was just as glad to give the part back. He'd just won a spot on the math team, and he was going to be so busy with practices that he'd barely be able to keep up with the small part he already had, much less take over the lead. So he was definitely off the list, too.

So was Kayla, for that matter. I realized that she'd only started doing props a few days earlier.

She hadn't even been around when the first pranks happened! My suspect list was shrinking fast. It looked as if Sal and TJ were the main ones left.

The lighting crew was doing some practicing that day, so for the first time we were getting an idea of what things would look like during a performance. They kept trying out different spotlights, sometimes cutting out the lights entirely for moments at a time. It was a little distracting, but Maddie said the crew needed to try things out with actors on the stage, so we just had to put up with it. I'm sure it was driving Sal and his crew crazy.

Watching from the wings, I was totally impressed with how well the actors were doing. They'd really been working hard on learning their lines, and I hardly ever had to prompt them. They were getting used to using their props, too. The play was really coming together, despite the fact that somebody didn't want it to happen. Maybe that certain somebody had given up by now, seeing that we weren't about to be stopped by silly pranks.

That's what I was thinking when it happened.

Right in the middle of Act One, Scene Four, during one of Nathan's monologues about how important his art was, the lights cut out for a couple of seconds. Nathan stopped talking, and everybody froze.

Everybody, that is, except for one person.

The person who pushed the art gallery flat over so that it nearly mashed me.

Chapter Twenty-one

The lights came back on just in time for me to see the flat rocking on its base, then starting to topple, then falling, as if in slow motion. I guess I must have screamed. It was like a wall was falling toward me, like something that would happen in an earthquake.

I heard pounding footsteps, and the next thing I knew I'd been grabbed and carried out of the way. Behind me, the flat crashed onto the little table I'd been sitting at.

"Are you okay?" Sal looked down at me, his face full of concern.

Sal. He was the one who'd rescued me. My head was spinning. Was this another act of sabotage? Was somebody trying to hurt me, put me out of commission? Keep me from finding out who they were?

If so, this was no prank. This was getting dangerous. I could have been badly hurt!

There was only one thing I was sure of: If Sal had run over to pull me out of the way, he *couldn't* have also been the one who pushed the flat over. Could he? Anyway, I saw the look in his eyes when he grabbed me. It was not the look of a destructive maniac. It was the look of someone desperate to save a . . . friend.

Sal helped me off the stage and walked me down to where Maddie was waiting. "Are you all right?" she asked, brushing my hair off my face. A crowd of kids clustered around. I saw Emma and TJ watching from the stage. TJ was frowning; he looked really upset.

"I'm fine, really," I said. "We should go on with rehearsal." I meant it. I really was fine. After all, nothing had happened. It had *almost* happened, but I'd been lucky. I was unhurt, and totally gressible[22].

"Are you sure?" Maddie asked.

"Positive." I knew I'd be talking to Miranda about this later, but for now there was no reason to waste the afternoon. "I just need my notebook," I said, suddenly feeling a little panicked. My stage manager's notebook! I hadn't let it out of my sight, except for loaning it to Ashleigh, since rehearsals had started. It had everything I needed, all the information about lines that had been changed, blocking, props — everything! Not to mention that it also contained my notes on the investigation Emma and Katherine and I had been doing.

---

[22]gressible: able to walk

135

"I'll get it!" said TJ, who was standing nearby, looking worried. He dashed up onto the stage and dashed back, carrying my book. He handed it over with a flourish. "There you go," he said.

"Thanks."

"All right," Maddie said, shooing the actors back up onto the stage. "Let's get on with it, then. Places!"

While I waited for everyone to settle back in to rehearsal, I flipped through my notebook, just to make sure everything was there. It all looked fine. The script, my stage manager notes, my little lists of props, my sheet of lighting cues . . . nothing was missing.

Then I looked in the back, just to check over my investigation notes again. Maybe I'd scratch Sal off the list then and there. He was my hero, not a suspect. Unless . . . could he have "saved" me as a way to cover his tracks? Argh! This was so confusing.

I found the page. And my heart skipped a beat. Scrawled over my SUSPECTS list, in red Magic Marker, were the words STOP SNOOPING — OR ELSE!

Chapter Twenty-two

There was no getting around it. The person who wanted to put a stop to the play was getting serious. And now the person had targeted me.

I snapped the notebook shut and stared up at the stage. TJ was up there, looking back at me. I felt a knot growing in my stomach.

If I thought about it, TJ was now the most likely suspect. He'd been in the background during every single incident. He had access to Mr. Wilson's room, where the green paint was kept. He knew all about electrical systems. I flashed on the way his face had looked after the flat almost fell on me. Was he upset because he was worried about me? Or because he thought I was about to identify him as the criminal? Finally — and thinking this made the knot grow even bigger — he'd tried to make friends with me, probably just to make me less suspicious.

I hated the idea that Katherine and Emma might be right about him. Why was that so upsetting to me? I barely knew the guy. Why should it matter if he turned out to be a jerk? Maybe I just couldn't stand the idea that I was a bad judge of character. I

thought TJ was funny and smart and talented —
and, well, cute. I couldn't deny that I'd started to
watch for him and notice when he walked into a
room. And, that day when we'd been pretending
to be Donna and Sam? I could blush just thinking
about it.

But it wasn't like I *liked* him. That would be a
huge mistake. A, because if he liked any Parker it
was definitely Katherine, and B, I had that deal
with my friends. No boy-craziness until at least
eighth grade. Not to mention C, because he might
be the destructive maniac I was chasing down.

Might be.

Couldn't be.

Could he?

It was time to find out more about TJ.

Which was why it was so perfect that he and I
ended up staying late that day, finishing up some
painting on the backdrop. Emma had dance, Sal
had "plans," and Maddie was headed for the police station to bring Miranda up to speed on the
latest events. Everybody had someplace to be, but
the background of the backdrop really had to be
finished that day. I may be artistically challenged,
but if there was one thing I'd learned to paint, it
was clouds. I could paint clouds for hours, no
problem. Especially if it meant I'd have some one-

on-one time with TJ. He agreed to stay late, too, when I told him Poppy would pick us up and bring us back to my house for supper when we were done.

The theater was dark, except for the light in the wings, where we were working. Oh, and the ghost light, the light near the costume closet. It was always on, night and day. Every theater has a ghost light, according to Maddie. It's a theater tradition to always keep one light burning.

It was quiet, too. Especially after all the chaos of rehearsal time. I was actually sort of enjoying the peacefulness of it all, dipping my long-handled paintbrush into the white paint and smearing it onto the canvas. We used the long handles so we could paint from a distance and not have to walk around on the freshly painted parts of the backdrop. It wasn't easy at first, but I got used to it.

I was enjoying the peacefulness, that is, until I realized that it might not be the brightest move for me to be alone in a dark theater with a boy who might quite possibly be the one who had tried to hurt me only a couple of hours earlier. Then, suddenly, the theater seemed dark and looming, and every little sound made me jump.

TJ seemed to notice my nervousness. "Don't

worry," he said with a little smile. "No scenery nearby to fall on you."

"It's not funny," I said.

"I never said it was," he answered.

"Where were you when it happened, anyway?" I asked casually, in my best Columbo style.

He shrugged. "Right here, I think. It all happened so fast."

"And you didn't see anything?"

"The lights were out, remember?" He shook his head. "Somebody moved quickly."

I looked around and calculated the distance from the backdrop to the flat that had fallen. That "somebody" could easily have been him.

We were quiet for a few moments. "So," I asked. "Tell me more about your old school. What was it like? Did you do theater there?"

"It was just a school." He moved away to get some more white paint.

"But did you have friends there?" I persisted. "You must have been sorry to leave so fast."

He looked at me. "Nope," he said flatly. "I wasn't sorry."

Hmm. Had he been kicked out? If so, why? And how could I find out? I decided to try the obvious way: Ask him. "Did you — *have* to leave?"

"What do you mean?" he asked, putting down

his brush and facing me. "What do you want to know, Ophelia? Just ask."

"I want to know why you left," I admitted. "Why you left so fast. Were you in trouble?"

"Me?" he asked, raising his eyebrows. Then he laughed. But it wasn't a happy laugh. "No, I wasn't in trouble."

"What, then?" I couldn't seem to quit.

"It's pretty simple," he said, sounding very angry all of a sudden. "My dad fell in love with my music teacher. My mom was jealous. They fought and fought and fought. Finally, my mom and I — we just left. We came here."

"You mean —" I was shocked. "Your parents are divorced?" I never would have guessed. I'd always assumed — he'd *let* me assume — he'd moved here with both parents.

"Not yet. But soon. That's all of it. Happy?"

I shook my head. "Of course not," I said. "I'm sorry, TJ. I really am." No wonder he'd been so secretive. It was obviously really painful for him to talk about what had happened with his parents.

"Why all the questions, anyway?" TJ asked. He still looked a little mad.

I shrugged. "Just wanted to get to know you better," I said. And as I said it, I discovered that it was true. It wasn't just my inner Columbo that wanted to know more about TJ. It was me. Ophelia. As far as I was concerned, TJ wasn't now and never had been a suspect. He was just a boy. A boy I found myself liking more and more. Unfortunately, that left me with no real suspects and an investigation that had gone nowhere. Not only that, it left me with an unrequited[23] crush.

That night at dinner, I watched TJ watching Katherine. Oh, sure, he talked and joked with Juliet and Helena and Viola, and discussed home improvement projects with Poppy, but I swear, every time I looked at him, he was looking at Katherine.

And you know what?

I was jealous.

---

[23]unrequited: one-sided, not returned

Chapter Twenty-three

That night, as I lay in bed waiting to fall asleep, I thought about it. I'd never really felt that kind of jealousy before. I mean, I was jealous in third grade when Emma made friends with Grace Walters. And I was jealous when it seemed like Jenny, who I always thought of as my cat, seemed to pick Juliet for her favorite for a few weeks. But this was a different kind of jealousy. Stronger. More painful. For the first time, I began to understand those lines in the play about how jealousy can eat you up.

I was going to have to let it go. I didn't want to like a boy that way, anyway. As soon as the play was over, I wouldn't be seeing TJ so often. I could forget about him and move on. Meanwhile, I would throw myself into working on the play. And I'd obviously have to start my investigation all over again.

That was my plan. And that was why I showed up early for the next rehearsal, ready to pitch in and finish off that backdrop, no matter what.

The regulars of stage crew were all there: TJ, Emma, and Sal. Plus Travis, who'd come to help again. We got right down to it while the actors rehearsed, putting out the paints and getting our brushes ready. The dropcloths — and our clothes — were covered with splotches of paint. That was nothing new. Painting is messy business.

There were white splotches from clouds and blue splotches from the sky and light green splotches from the meadow and brown splotches from the cows.

But suddenly, I spotted a splotch of another color. A splotch of metallic green. In a place I would never, in a million years, have expected to see it.

Chapter Twenty-four

I stared. I couldn't help myself.

Suddenly, it all came together.

"Are you okay?" TJ asked. My face must have gone white.

"Sure, sure," I said. "I mean — no. I think I need a drink. Or something." I put down my brush.

"Want me to come with you?" Emma asked.

I nodded. She handed her brush to TJ and followed me offstage and out into the hall.

"What's the matter?" she asked. "You look terrible."

"Thanks," I said, trying to smile. "Em, you're not going to believe this. Guess what I just saw? A splotch of green metallic paint."

"Huh?" She looked like she thought I was nuts. "Where?"

I knew she wouldn't believe me if I told her, so I didn't answer. "This is it," I said. "Now I know who it was. That paint matches exactly with the paint on the signs, and the notes, and the backdrop. There's no question about it." I was almost talking to myself.

"Ophelia, where's the paint? Who's the sus-

145

pect?" Emma was practically jumping up and down with excitement.

I shook my head. "Just for now, maybe it's better if you don't know. I want you to go back in there and act like there's nothing wrong," I said. "I have to set a trap so I can prove what I suspect. Let me think." I paced up and down the hall, knowing that any minute Maddie was going to want to start rehearsal. We didn't have any time to waste. Emma paced up and down, too, but she was just staring at me as if I'd gone crazy. "Okay," I said. "I've got it. Just go back and keep on painting. And when I come in, just play along with what I do."

Chapter Twenty-five

It was pretty easy, in the end. I ran to my locker to find the card I'd bought for everyone to sign for Maddie on opening night. We were going to give her flowers, too. Ashleigh had tipped me off that the cast and crew usually did that.

Then I made a phone call to Miranda.

I headed back to the auditorium, my heart beating fast. Just outside the door, I stopped to take a few deep breaths. The important thing was for me to act casual.

"Hey, guys," I said when I came back. "Sorry about that. I skipped lunch today, and I guess I was just hungry." I pulled the card out of its paper bag. "Listen, as long as Maddie's not here, I'm going to pass this around for everybody to sign. Want to be the first ones?" I handed the card and a pen to Emma, giving her a special look.

She played along, just as I'd asked her to, signing her name with a flourish. Then she passed the card to Sal. He took a few moments to think of something to say, and my heart started beating overtime again. Any minute now, Maddie was going to arrive and ask me to call the actors to rehearsal.

Finally, Sal scribbled a few words, signed the card, and passed it along to TJ. I guess having only initials for a name means you sign pretty fast; before I knew it the card was in Travis's hands.

Travis paused. "Should I sign?" he asked, looking over at me. "I'm not really officially a part of this whole thing." He waved a hand around.

"Of course," I said. My voice sounded squeaky. I cleared my throat. "You've helped so much. Officially or not, you're on the crew."

He smiled, nodded, signed quickly, and gave the card back to me.

"Thanks!" I said lightly, tucking it back into the bag. "I'm going to get some other signatures. Back in a sec." I walked out of their sight. I opened the bag. Flipped the card open. And stared down at one of the signatures. "You're the best!" it said above the name.

The S looked like a 5. Just what I'd figured.

I had my proof.

There was only one more thing to do.

Chapter Twenty-six

I'd called "five minutes." I'd called "places." And rehearsal was just about to start. Everybody was on hand: Sarabeth and Nathan were onstage. The other actors were in the audience, waiting for their cues. Sal and his crew were in the wings, putting the final touches on the backdrop. Even some of the lighting guys were there.

I was all set up at my little table in the wings. From where I sat, now that the flat that had almost beaned me had been moved, I could see Travis, TJ, and Emma bending over to paint clouds. I took a deep breath. It was time to expose our prankster.

"Maddie?" I called down to her. "Before we start, I just want to work on a blocking problem. It's from Act Two, Scene Two, the one between Sam and Veronica. I'd like to act it out, show Nathan and Katherine where they're going wrong, if that's okay."

Maddie looked a little puzzled, but she nodded. "Sure."

I pretended to look around. "I need someone to help me out here. Hey, how about you, Travis?" I asked. I grabbed him before he could protest and brought him over to the center of the stage. I stuck a script into his hands, opened to the right page, and pointed to his lines. "We'll start here," I said. I didn't give him a chance to read ahead. I just jumped in with Veronica's line.

"'But Sam, I found this letter!'" I said, holding up the card everyone had signed. "'I know all about Donna. You're still in love with her, aren't you? *Aren't* you?'"

Travis looked at me. I saw something in his eyes. Fear? Panic? But then it disappeared, as quickly as it had come, and he was confident Travis again. He gave me that slow smile.

Then he looked down and read his lines. "'Oh, Veronica, can't you forget about it? Jealousy is a bitter, terrible emotion that does nobody any good. It'll eat you up inside, make you do things you'll regret.'"

"'Make you do things you'll regret,'" I echoed. I paused for a moment to take a deep breath. The time had come. "Isn't that the truth, Travis? That jealousy can eat you up, make you do things you'll regret?" I reached into my pocket and pulled out my copy of the note he'd written the day he'd pulled the fire alarm. I held it up so he could see it.

"What's that?" he asked, acting innocent.

"I think you know," I said. "And I think everybody else will know, too, when they compare the handwriting on this note to your signature on this card. And when they see the green paint on your shirttail." That's where I'd seen the splotch. It was just a tiny spot, and it never would have shown except that Travis had untucked his otherwise perfectly white shirt while we were painting.

"You're nuts!" he cried, throwing down the script and hurriedly tucking in his shirt.

"Ophelia! What's going on?" asked Maddie from the audience. "This isn't in the script."

I didn't answer. I was following my *own* script by then. "You couldn't stand it, could you? Watching Sarabeth pretending to be in love with somebody else made you so jealous. So you wrote some threatening notes, pulled some pranks in hopes that we'd give up and the play wouldn't happen. But we didn't give up. And then Sarabeth broke up with you, which just made you angry on top of everything. You wanted to get even."

"This is ridiculous!" shouted Travis. "You can't prove it."

I knew I was right. I remembered Travis's face that day when Sarabeth said she was going to run lines with Nathan. Plus, the handwriting. I'd never seen Travis's writing before, because he never filled in an audition sheet. But his signature on the card for Maddie gave him away. It all added up. I had no doubts.

"You got the paint from Mr. Wilson's shop," I went on. "And probably the tool, too, the one you used to slash the backdrop. You blew the fuse, and pulled the fire alarm, and you pushed that flat over onto me."

"I didn't mean that!" he cried. "I didn't know you were there! I never meant to *hurt* anyone!"

"Travis?" Sarabeth stood up from her seat in the audience and began walking toward the stage. "It was *you*?"

"I never put that tack in your shoe, babe!" Travis gave her a pleading look. "I *especially* never meant to hurt you!"

That's when it seemed to dawn on Travis that he'd just pretty much admitted it. He slumped over into the chair and put his head in his hands.

I guess I should have felt victorious. But I didn't. I felt sorry for him.

Chapter Twenty-seven

Dress rehearsal was a total disaster.

Actors forgot not only their lines and their blocking but their entrances and exits. Props got messed up so that when Nathan went to pick up the phone there was a flowerpot there instead, and when he went to get the newspaper he came back with a phone. (He got big laughs from the audience, but remember, this play isn't a comedy.) Stage crew put the football game setup where there was supposed to be a kitchen. The makeup people didn't quite have it together, so some of the actors looked a little washed-out while others looked like they were ready for Halloween.

Oh, and did I mention that there was a huge snowstorm so we almost didn't have dress rehearsal at all?

Anyway, just about everything that could go wrong *did* go wrong. And this time, we couldn't blame Travis. He'd been suspended from school for a week and forbidden to come anywhere near the auditorium. I still felt a tiny bit sorry for him, but once I'd heard Sarabeth's side of the story, I began to understand why she broke up with him. It turned out that his jealousy had been getting worse and worse until it was nearly out of control. Sarabeth said Travis would get upset if she even talked to another guy in the halls! She'd had enough, she told us. And she confessed that she'd had a tiny suspicion that he might be the one pulling the pranks. She had hoped that he would stay away from the play if she broke up with him, but instead it just made him angrier and more jealous.

Anyway, as I said, dress rehearsal was a total disaster. But Maddie reassured us after it was all over. "This is totally normal," she said. "Theater tradition says that a bad dress rehearsal means a good opening night. So would you really have wanted things to go perfectly tonight?"

Well, maybe. Just so I would know that they *could* go perfectly. I went home after rehearsal feeling more nervous than ever about my debut as a stage manager. I was going to be responsible for opening night!

At a quarter to nine that night the phone rang. It was Emma. "I know we can't talk long," she said. She knows about my parents' rule: no phone calls after nine. "But I *had* to tell you. You'll never believe who's downstairs." She was whispering into the phone, and I could picture her in her room, sitting cross-legged on her bed.

"Who?" I asked.

"Sal and Maddie!"

"*What*? Are you kidding?" I couldn't believe my ears.

Emma giggled. "I know! It's wild. They came by — get this — to tell my mom and dad what the play is about. I guess they realized that my parents would be coming and decided it would be fair to let them know ahead of time. I listened from the landing on the stairs."

"But —" How could Emma be giggling? "What about your mom and Sal?" I asked.

"That's history!" She sounded really happy. "They laughed about how the play makes it seem so dramatic. And my dad already knew the whole story. Sal only told Maddie about a week ago; before that, he didn't want to mess up his chances with her. But now that they're a couple —"

"Wait! Sal and Maddie are a couple?" I couldn't keep up.

"Oh, definitely," Emma said. "You should see them together when they're away from school. Holding hands, staring into each other's eyes, the whole thing."

"What about your parents?" I asked. She'd been so worried about them.

"They're okay," Emma answered. "I think my dad was feeling overwhelmed at work or something. But they aren't fighting so much these days."

"Ophelia!" called my mom from downstairs. I knew what that meant. "Gotta go," I told Emma. "See you tomorrow. Opening night!"

"Break a leg," she said. "Don't worry, you're going to be awesome."

I don't know if I was awesome, but the show was. Maddie turned out to be right. We must have gotten all the mistakes out of our systems during dress rehearsal, because on opening night the show went perfectly, from the moment the curtain went up (on my command!) to the final applause. The actors got a standing ovation when they came out for curtain calls, and the applause grew even louder when the cast presented Maddie with a bouquet of white roses.

The audience was still filing out when I saw TJ walking backstage, holding a single, long-stemmed red rose. He was headed straight for Katherine, who was talking excitedly with Nathan and Sarabeth. I felt that little jealous spark flare up, and I turned away so I wouldn't have to see him give it to her.

Then there was a tap on my shoulder. "I thought you deserved a flower, too," TJ said, holding out the rose.

"For me?" I asked.

"You did great," he told me. "You *are* great. I really like you, Ophelia." He looked straight at me when he said that.

"But —" I shook my head. "I thought you liked Katherine."

He looked shocked. "What? No way! Your sister is *not* my type."

"But you always stare at her." I couldn't seem to let it go.

He laughed. "I'm just trying to figure her out. How she does it, you know? She's kind of fascinating. But *like* her? That way? Not in a million years."

Suddenly, it was sinking in. TJ liked me. That way. I didn't know what to say, what to think. So I just said, "Thanks, TJ. For the flower." I raised it to my face and sniffed. It smelled heavenly.

"Thelonius Jefferson," said TJ.

"What?" I asked. The smell of the rose had kind of fogged my brain.

"That's what my initials stand for. You're the first person I've ever told."

Wow. "Thanks," I said again.

"And if you *ever* tell anyone else . . ." he began with a smile.

"I won't," I interrupted. I saw Emma coming toward us, a huge smile on her face. I had to talk

quickly. "But TJ, I don't know if I'm ready for —
you know."

"Are you ready to be friends?" he asked. "That's
all I'm asking right now."

That was easy. "Definitely," I told him. He
reached out, took my hand, and squeezed it, looking into my eyes the whole time.

"Hey, you guys!" Emma said. TJ dropped my
hand. "Wasn't that awesome?" She held up both
hands for high fives, and we smacked palms. "We
did it!"

"We did it!" TJ and I echoed.

We really did.

So, was our play cursed because Poppy had said
the name of that — other play? It might have
seemed like it for a while. But in the end, I'd have
to say it wasn't. And I think my new friend Thelonius Jefferson would agree.